MW00897744

# DRIVE-BY

## An Inner City Novel

C. Yusef Wells

Edited By

TeErra J. Johnson

Let us not forget…the homeless, the helpless, the hospitalized, the hungry, the sick, the poor, the incarcerated, the oppressed, orphans, travelers without a home, and believers all over the universe.

All thanks and praise to the Creator of all the worlds for bestowing me with the ability to embark on this writing.

A special tribute to my mother whose prayers for me and all mothers who have worried about their children…May their tears be a river in Paradise…. and their laughter the life of the party.

And prop's to a few people who have inspired and/or assisted me on this journey:

Robert "Bobby" Poole

Robert Dellinger

Donald Bakeer

Alexander Folk

TeErra Johnson

Kimberly Williams

Jimmy Johnson

Latashia Holmes

"Scooby Taylor"

Nathaniel "Rollo" Taylor

Fantastic Designs

Myla Twillie

C.T. Taylor

# CONTENTS

# Chapter 1

## SECRET POLICE

A canvass-covered military truck navigated through the narrow back roads of a South African Township. Rocks and mud greeted the tires at a vigorous rate of speed, which created an extremely bumpy ride for it's passengers who were familiar with this urban area, but seemingly different in the dark of night. Their roving eyes would occasionally catch a glimpse of uncut crops and shabby tin-roofed shacks between the cracks in the canopy. When the sound of the wheels rotating through the slush finally hit a low gear, the passengers knew they were close. With deadly intentions the hit-squad approached a land clearance where four suspected Anti-Apartheid rebels were huddled around a barrel of fire. They had finally found their target. Engulfed in chatter, the rebels were unaware that they had been spotted by their enemy, a small unit of South African Secret Police, who had trekked several miles through several villages in search of them. Now it was too late.

Adrenaline gushed through the unit's veins. Their hearts raced as the vehicle decelerated to a creeping crawl. Under cover of a few trees and brush they snapped magazine clips into assault weapons and held them with intense grips.

The driver commanded at a tone just above a whisper, "Take your positions Commandos!"

Within their sights were illuminated ebony faces, with ivory teeth and the white of shocked eyes as the brakes screeched. The rebel's heads jerked in the direction of the truck. Swiftly the canvass elevated. A rapid fire assault spit light on bullet-riddled bodies!

The unit smiled and exchanged high-fives as the smoke-filled truck sped off with a rancid smell of gunfire trailing it into the depth of night.

*\*\**

As the moon departed from the Eastern hemisphere, it was welcomed on the West. The night's star shined upon a lone dark sedan with deep-tinted windows, zipping thru traffic like a heat-seeking missile. Off the main highway and into the heart of South Central, it dipped and swerved recklessly into a residential section.

Headlights clicked off. After bending two corners, it decelerated to a slow cruise, halting directly in front of an on-going teenage party. Electric windows slid down in unison. A thunderous voice was projected from the sedan and heard just over the sound of their music.

"BLUE HERE FOOLS!"

Before anyone could process what was unfolding, a vicious volley of gunfire erupted. Bullets chased moving shadows that scrambled for their survival. The sedan sped off, leaving behind a rancid cloud of gunsmoke and burnt rubber as it dissolved from the scene of screams and fallen bodies.

Minutes later, the car's engine still ran hot from its mission around the city. The three occupants drove further away from the scene while bursting with laughter. As they delighted in their egregious acts, a badge twinkled on and off the driver's heaving chest. Neon lights from the passing cars would occasionally display the name 'Captain Starks' engraved in metal.

In the midst of their celebration, Captain Starks turned to Sergeant Burger in the passenger seat, "Did you observe those low-life subjects scatter and hit the deck?"

"DAMN RIGHT I DID!"

Officer Faulk rose up from the back, "Captain! Next weekend we'll be Southsiders and target a Northside party...or West or East!"

"What about it Captain," Sergeant Burger pressed, "do we keep their black asses at war or do we attack the barrios of those bean-eating Mexicans?"

Like a flick of a switch, the Captain snatched his hand from the wheel, his finger aiming directly towards the Sergeant's face, "Sergeant Burger!" he yelled, maneuvering so fast that he almost swerved into another car. He centered back on the road and picked up where he left off, still boiling, "Keep dissension stirred between every creature you encounter. Everyone except those of Aryan descent! Red, brown, yellow black, Jews, and sympathetic whites who mingle with the enemies!"

"Yourself and Officer Faulk back there need to start compiling information from the streets. Get addresses from your informants. Ignite fuel to the fire! They must never have peace with one another!"

"Yeah!" Sergeant Burger rallied along, "Dead or divided."

The captain grew more passionate by the minute. He channeled this sick energy into his foot and put more force against the gas pedal. As his fury grew, so did the speed of the sedan.

# Chapter 2

## THE ABANDONED FACTORY

Elsewhere in the neighborhood, teenagers of all ages continued their nightly routines. Some ran the streets while others were involved in more constructive ventures.

Young Ginger Davis stood on the front porch of her girlfriend's home, with her back to the boulevard. At nearly seventeen years of age, she had the spirit of a Wiseman and the heart of a lion, with unshakable ambition.

"Bye Dee-Dee, it was fun flirting with the future," Ginger said, speaking into the screen door.

Dee-Dee giggled, "It really was. You a prominent judge then politician, me, the doctor and eventual Surgeon General."

"Imagine that," Ginger said with a shy smile. She drifted off for a moment, thinking of all the possibilities, the type of life she could live, and the amount of influence she could have.

In the midst of her gaze, she was distracted by a familiar aroma. Her nose was welcomed to the smell of fried chicken coming from Dee-Dee's kitchen and passing right through the screen door. This reminded her of dinner with her mother, she then said her farewells and darted on her way towards home.

She spun around and jumped off the porch, walked through the gate and onto the pavement. Time truly flies when you're having fun, Ginger thought as she headed towards the Eastside projects.

Her brisk walk advanced to a jog as she became more conscious of the night's hour. Now she raced home. She shifted towards a shortcut through an abandoned factory. Her tennis shoes beat against the pavement and cracks in the concrete.

"Come on legs. Gotta get home before Momma eats dinner," Ginger said aloud, as though her legs had ears of their own.

Bending down, Ginger stepped through a hole in the fence that surrounded the factory's perimeter. She darted across the parking lot, turned toward the rear wall of the factory and stopped dead in her tracks.

Moments prior, the black sedan whipped into an alley which led to the entrance grounds of the same abandoned factory. Just as it parked next to an awaiting vice car, the dirty cops jumped out and saw that a red flag had emerged into their blueprint – Ginger.

Ginger's gaped mouth hung wide open in pure shock. The captain's militant face, square jaw, and beady eyes locked on Ginger. Slowly, he dabbed at the remaining smudge on his face and gestured toward her like a villain on the prowl.

Ginger was frozen in grave danger. For a split second, time stood still. Her image was that of a faceless clock. Swiftly she shifted her stare from the captain, to the dark sedan, to the other officers, then back to the captain's stunned mug.

The Captain yelled, "Grab her! Don't let her get away!"

Ginger slipped the grasp of the first officer. Her victory wasn't acknowledged for long because after her swift escape, she entered a foot chase in full pursuit by all three policemen.

She didn't know who was chasing her, but Ginger instinctively knew that she had fallen into the wrong place at the wrong time. And now, she had to run for her life. Her mind raced just as quickly as her feet. Over a fence, through a backyard and around the corner, she gasped for breath in search of refuge. The sound of boots hitting the ground was just a short distance behind.

After another left turn and then a right, Ginger stumbled upon the sound of gospel music. This led her to a huge door with a cross hanging above the entrance. The congregation of churchgoers who were singing and clapping, fully engrossed in the late night service, didn't see Ginger running in and blending amongst the crowd.

Panting, Ginger's chest contracted rapidly. She finally got a second to breathe. Ginger strategically slumped down on the middle of the pew, sandwiched between two extra heavy-set elderly women. They stood and shouted 'Yes Preacher!' and 'Amen' devoutly, too focused on the theatrical sermon to pay much attention to her.

Just on the other side of the church wall, the winded men frantically peered into the side windows. They could barely make out any clear figures. Stained glass paintings blurred their view and the fellowshipping congregation caused too much of a distraction.

"I don't see her!" the captain huffed, too exhausted to stand up. Instead, he bent over, palms pressed against his knees, resting his weight evenly.

After one last look through the window, Captain Starks delivered his final ruling to the officers, "It is a safe assumption that she can't positively I.D. either one of us. Also, we're a good five miles or so from the drive-by."

"I think we just scared the shit out of her," Sergeant Burger managed to say while trying to catch his breathe. He wiped the back of his hand along his forehead and noticed his sweat was mixed with black residue, "Some of the smudge is still on our faces," still breathing heavily.

To fit the characters in their hidden plot, the cops wore smudge, made up of brownish and black toned make-up. Ultimately, under their bandanas, it was the smudge that saved them from being totally revealed.

The captain gave a sinister smile, "Yes…the damn black face."

The men returned to their night, satisfied that they still accomplished their mission despite the encounter with Ginger.

# Chapter 3

## VICTIM OR VICTOR

The following morning, sunlight pierced through Ginger's bedroom window in the projects with radiant authority. Crazy nights with open endings had become normalized; living in this neighborhood was simply unpredictable. Ginger tried not to think about the mysterious events that occurred just hours before she woke up. Today was her big day. She had to get dressed for a summer job interview.

Hurriedly, she primped in a full-length mirror behind the bedroom door. Every curl on her short-cropped hair was laid in place. Almond eyes twinkled with approval as she inspected her petite frame and silky golden brown complexion.

She took a quick glance at the clock hanging on the wall. If she left the house now, she could arrive to the office early enough to make a good impression. After one final look, Ginger rushed through a short narrow hallway and into the kitchen. She found her mother sitting over a cup of coffee, watching a small television set on the breakfast table.

Ginger bent to plant a kiss on her mother's cheek, "Bye Momma, I'm running late…don't want to miss my bus."

"Be careful baby. Come straight home after the interview. The streets are so dangerous these days," her mother said, pursing her lips for another sip.

"I will Momma," laying a tender palm on her mother's shoulder. "Please, Momma, don't worry. I'll be alright…"

In a timely coincidence, her mother pointed to the television. She noticed a familiar house that was several blocks away from their apartment on the news. She almost spilled her coffee reaching for the remote to turn up the volume.

"Once again, the inner city was plagued with violence last night. A hail of bullets interrupted a teenage party on East Forty Second Street at approximately nine thirty P.M."

The news anchor gripped her mic, "The apparent gang-related shooting was the one hundred and tenth such incident reported this year. Three young males were killed. From eyewitness accounts, a dark, late model sedan with tinted windows pulled in front of the party. The occupants shouted gang slogans and opened fire."

Sedan…sedan…sedan… Ginger instantly had a flashback: whirling repetition of the captain's face, the dark sedan, the other officers, and flashes of a typical drive-by shooting.

She stared at the set in a trance-like state.

"The names of the victims are being withheld due to their ages and pending notifications to their parents. Los Angeles police Chief Morgan urges anyone with knowledge of the suspects to come forward or anonymously contact Homicide Detective Morales at 555-HELP. This is Sharon Page reporting from South Central Los Angeles."

Her mother's finger was still erect, pointing at the T.V., "See what I mean Gingee…Just be real careful child."

Ginger snapped back from her reverie and uttered softly, "Bye Momma, I'll be home just before dark."

When she reached the front door and closed it shut, she hoped to do the same with her flashbacks. She tried her best to unconsciously tuck and smother the night away. Her only focus was to get this job and save up enough to move her and her mother out the projects. She hated seeing her mother work so hard all her life, only to come home to a neighborhood that could be mistaken for a battlefield at times.

Swiftly, Ginger moved through those same projects. Morning dew rested on the grass scattered with beer bottles, old furniture, and occasionally, a diaper or two. Ginger grimaced at the sight. Glancing over her shoulder, she spied a half-dozen boys squatting down, rolling craps on the ground. They bounced and shook as if they were imitating the dice they threw.

Some were older but most of them were around her age. One noticed Ginger walking up. After the first set of eyes led, the others followed. Fully distracted as Ginger approached, they stopped their game, stood and struck macho poses.

The boys began to cat-call in unison, "Hey Gingee...Babyeeee!"

She shook her head with disgusting disapproval at the early bird gamblers. Knowing this wasn't their desired response, Ginger forced a smile and acknowledged them with a brisk fan of her hand. She hoped this would appease their egos, only then would they allow her to walk in peace. She happily scooted past them and quickened her pace.

You never knew what to expect around this area, day or night. It was one obstacle after another. Ginger's attention was focused on a group of girls, mingling and giggling at the opening of the projects near the bus stop.

The sight of Lil Bit, Dynasty, and D'Zine always meant trouble. She planted a stern frown on her forehead. Her expression softened, as she spotted Big Tasha not too far off. Big Tasha was the girls' gang leader and Ginger's only true friend in the projects.

The girls started to advance toward Ginger. This triggered her defense mechanisms. Any other time she could deal with them, but today, she had somewhere to be.

"Well, if it ain't Miss Goodie-do-Right." Lil Bit said as they blocked her path.

Through the corner of Ginger's eye, she watched the bus as it drove past her stop. This infuriated her even more. She cocked her fists on her narrow hip, tightened her lips, and was ready for battle. This edged them on further.

"All properly dolled up!" Lil Bit sassed.

The girls scowled at Ginger's professional attire, it agitated them to the core.

Dynasty stepped forward, "Yeah, where you going…to a square-bitch convention?"

"Get out of my way! You don't intimidate me, Dynasty. Not you Lil Bit, or D'Zine either. None of you do. You never have and you never will!" Ginger declared, rolling her eyes.

"Awhh shit! We real hard today…huh" D'Zine chuckled.

"But not hard enough to hang out with us. I can't stand yo' ass!" Dynasty yelled. She parked directly in front of Ginger, looking her dead in the eye, "I should bomb yo' damn face."

Ginger stood her ground and planted a foot backwards to declare she was ready. She balled up a fist.

Immediately, Big Tasha muscled her way between them before the first punch was thrown, "Stall that shit out! Ya'll know Gingee ain't with it like we are. She don't gang bang, so quit fucking with her."

Dynasty backed off, pointing a firm finger in Ginger's face, "One day, she won't save yo' good, law-abiding ass," applying her venomous stare.

"Yeah…right, tramp…Tell it walking." Ginger yelled, as the girls moved on.

Big Tasha and Ginger walked toward the bus stop. Ginger tried to shake it off, for now. But she knew the girls were bound to be a problem again.

"Thanks Tasha, you always pop-up at the right time."

"Yeah…I'm knowing. They're mostly mouth. But they're home girls and you are too, and I ain't having no fighting amongst our own, especially over attitudes. Now, where you going?"

"On a job interview."

It was like she was living in two worlds at once. One, she wanted to get away from, and the other, was out there waiting for her to live in it.

"I wonder if I'll ever get where you're at one day? Nawhh...I'm caught up. I love these projects. Banging is too deep in my heart. Probably always will be."

Ginger pointed to Big Tasha's chest, "All that can be put into a more positive channel Tasha. Drop some hope on it."

"I'll give it some thought. I just might cross that gangsta bridge one of these days. Meanwhile, here comes your bus. Stay safe."

"You too...And thanks again," Ginger extended her arms, giving Big Tasha a warm embrace.

Big Tasha laughed, "Quit mentioning it."

***

Ginger sat across from a desk, in an office located in the financial district. She tried her best to hide her nervous nature under a smile.

A gray haired women in a fashionable navy business suit peered over her butterfly-framed bifocals, "Miss Davis...Upon review of your application, our firm took note and paid special attention to your keyboard ability. We were also impressed with your I.Q. score."

Ginger's confidence sprouted, ripening her posture, "Thank you ma'am. I've been typing since I was nine years old."

"Can you operate a computer?"

Ginger had an even better answer, "My memory is photographic. If you show me once, you won't have to show me a second time."

"I like your optimistic nature." The woman was quite impressed, "I'm going to hire you. As you know, the position is temporary for the duration of the summer. The pay is minimum wage."

She shuffled through a stack of papers, "However, upon high school graduation and pending your ability to adapt, we will convert your status to permanent with a negotiable increase in wages. Is this satisfactory with you?"

Ginger was overwhelmed, "Why yes...of course."

\*\*\*

A joyful Ginger rode homeward-bound on public transportation. She passed the time by thinking quietly to herself about her new job. At one of the bus stops, two young boys dressed in gang gear boarded. They wore the usual, jeans, tennis shoes, T-shirt and baseball cap that reflected the color of their set.

The first one trotted down the narrow aisle, arrogantly. When he got close, he grabbed the handrail next to Ginger, swung his body and flopped down in the seat behind her. The second followed.

The braver of the two mistakenly asked, "What's up, freak-mama?"

Ginger saw this coming from a mile away. "First of all, there ain't nothing odd or abnormal about my nature. Second of all...nothing could ever be up with me and you," she said sharply.

The dynamics instantly changed. His demeanor sunk and humiliation lingered.

15

"Awhh, man! Baby sister just officially clowned yo' ass. You been properly put in place." His friend teased, with a pointed finger and rolling jokes, laughing and bouncing in the seat next to him.

He couldn't bear the embarrassment. He tightened his jaw and swelled his chest. There was no way he could go out like that and return home. He had to have the last word, at least in front of his boy.

"The tack-head dame is tripping with her uppity-ass."

Ginger turned around, staring him face-to-face, "Uppity? You need to raise them pants. And elevate your mind while you're at it. You evidently possess a very low degree of self-esteem. If you loved and respected yourself, you could love and respect your people!"

The feistiness was exposed. She even caused a few heads to turn a couple of seats away.

His friend continued to instigate, adding fuel to their opposing fires, "Damn! What's up with that homie?"

"Nothing! Just like she ain't nothing, I seen her around," nodding his head. "She stay in the 'jects' with my cousin, Dynasty."

Ginger rolled her eyes in response, turned, forward and tuned them out. Her inability to react infuriated him even more. And that was all it took. This was a dangerous recipe for someone full of youthful energy, with nothing to lose. He wanted revenge. He rode the rest of the way in silence, plotting.

After a few more stops, the boys got off the bus. Pulsating from pent up anger, he entered a phone booth on the next block and planted a vengeful seed.

16

"Yeah, Dynasty, she straight dissed me!" He yelled into the receiver, "She's on her way home right now!"

***

Ginger finally made it to her side of town. After she got off the bus, she trotted down the walkway of the projects. Her pace was rather quick, anxious to inform her mother about the good news of her job offer. Step by step, she became even more excited.

Midway home, the worst of the worst happened. It took her a second to make out their faces but by that time, it was too late. Ugh, it's them, again! Lil Bit, D'Zine, and Dynasty swung around a breezeway and accosted her.

Armed with a knife, Dynasty lunged toward Ginger with deadly force. Ginger's instincts clicked. She grabbed her attacking arm and with her free hand, she pulled Dynasty to the ground by her hair, just as her uncle had taught her.

The yanking did not cease when their flesh greeted concrete. The hairstyle Dynasty wore was now unrecognizable. It was clenched tightly in Ginger's fist, squeezed in between her knuckles. They wrestled on the ground like wild animals and squirmed about recklessly. A punch here, a jab there. Yank. Yank. And pull. Real ghetto warfare.

They rolled over several times with Lil Bit and D'Zine in the background, cheering Dynasty on. The girls couldn't actually make out who was winning the fight amidst all the scuffling. But they had no doubt about who would ultimately win. In their minds, it was Ginger who was the weak one. It was Ginger who couldn't hold her own. It was Ginger who had walked into the den of wolves. And Dynasty was their alpha, there was no way the outcome wouldn't be in her favor.

Suddenly, the commotion stopped. Their eyes widened and their hyping ceased. Ginger slowly rose to her feet. Her foe lied motionless in a small puddle of blood. The moment was too heavy to bear. Ginger remained still. The victim had become the victor.

Her fingers relaxed themselves. They released the weapon that was originally intended to harm her. Clink! Clink! The sound of the knife hitting the ground opened up a floodgate of questions. How did I get here? What's going to happen to me? What would come of my future now? Have the streets finally pulled me in?

Ginger's mind raced from north to south, and back to square one. She replayed different scenarios in her head, plastered and frozen in time. A knife was at her feet. Blood. An injured girl. And two eyewitnesses.

*** 

That evening, the projects riddled with squad cars and flashing red lights. Sirens screamed over the constant chatter. People were abundant, and their curiosity was even greater. An ambulance moved through the crowd, as if it were parting the Red Sea. After everyone got out of the way, Ginger was seen handcuffed and escorted to a police vehicle. This was a sight all too familiar in this area.

Amongst the surrounding chaos, a short and stubby officer wrote out the police report with a pen in hand. Unfortunately for Ginger, D'Zine and Lil Bit happened to be the prime witnesses for the case.

"She jumped us for no reason!" Lil Bit yelled, exaggerating their encounter to the fullest. Her pulsating adrenaline heightened the situation, implanting grave falsities.

D'Zine went along with the lie, "That's right! Ginger Davis did it! She stabbed Dynasty," projecting loudly, capturing even more attention from the crowd.

They were in cahoots. Their bias argument wasn't shy to the lips. They were going to protect their friend and abide by loyalty. It was their testimony that would make all the difference. Ginger was going down.

The agitated officer raised his palm to the halt position, "Calm it down! If not, we can all go to the precinct for your statements."

The girls settled. Through their wrestling tension, he continued the procedure and noted everything in his notepad.

# Chapter 4

## THE VERDICT

Ginger and her mother sat anxiously in an interview room in front of Mrs. Closky, a court appointed public defender. The three were hosting a conference at juvenile hall to address the stabbing incident. Ginger tried to remain calm and stoic in character. She needed to be strong now, more than ever.

"You have been detained here at the hall, due to the severe nature of the charge against you," Mrs. Closky said, with an heir of presumption.

"It's been three days now. I have a job to report to. And I keep telling you that I was the intended victim!" Ginger fumed in her seat. Deep regret was accompanied by dried blood spatter, resting on her white-collared shirt and grey suit. Both of which had festered for over seventy-two hours in a holding room. Her suit was no longer freshly ironed and her shirt was far from white.

"My Gingee would never do such a thing. How come no one believes her? And why can't she be released to me until this thing is straightened out?" Mrs. Davis asked.

"I'm very sorry Mrs. Davis, but I have no control over the detention. I am here to assist your daughter with legal issues directly related to the case." Mrs. Closky tried to keep her tone at bay, even with all the emotional distress staring back at her from the other side of the table.

She turned to face Ginger, "Your charge is very sever young lady. Fortunately, the girl lived…just barely."

Ginger huffed and slumped deeply into the seat. It was like she couldn't breathe. Whether it was fury or disbelief, Ginger reached her boiling point. She jolted her body forward and slammed her open hands down on the desk, "It was an accident! I was only trying to defend myself!"

Mrs. Closky flinched briefly, unphased by Ginger's reaction. She had seen it all in the twenty years she practiced law.

"The reports reflect statements from two eyewitnesses: Linda 'Lil Bit' Sanders and D'Zine Jones. They positively identify you as the assailant, Miss Davis." She dropped her head to skim through more documents before looking back up, "From a legal viewpoint, we do not have a defensive leg to stand on. At best, we might have the mercy of the court. And the fact that you do not possess a prior record. Anything your friend Tasha would say would be hearsay."

"This is all wrong…" Mrs. Davis mumbled, "Lawd knows it's wrong." Tears crept to the corner of her eyes. They were forced to expose themselves, sliding down her cheek from their hiding place.

Ginger looked to her mother and quivered inside. She searched her brain for an answer. She tried to think as quickly as possible before getting bogged down by the emotional weight she was experiencing and putting her mother through.

21

"Can I have a jury trial? Maybe they will believe me." Ginger pleaded.

"No, Miss Davis. All juvenile offenses are heard either by a judge or a commissioner. It's called a court trial. The exception to the rule are juveniles who are tried as adults. And you do not want to be tried as an adult. Trust me…"

Mrs. Closky inhaled deeply. The professional face she wore was melting. At first, she had a few reservations about Ginger's case. But seeing her in person and hearing her story changed all of that. She didn't want to see this young girl punished for an act of self-defense, nor any child for that matter.

"The system is detaining everyone who has violence attached to their charges. Violence is rampant and the courts are being very harsh."

She finished her statement with a subtle sigh of sympathy, hoping her change of demeanor wasn't noticeable to her clients. She hated when her sensitive nature showed up at work. But this job poked at her wounds. After years of schooling and practicing law, she still was affected by the people. The stories. The misfortune. The cycle. Each time, it stripped her from the monogamous procedures and reminded her why she signed up in the first place. She hated when a child got lost in the system. She was once that child.

The innate maternal protector rose out of Mrs. Davis, "Please do something for my baby!, she yelled feverishly. By this point, tears stained her face generously. They hadn't seemed to stop flowing since they began.

Ginger's mother had had enough. There was no way she would let her only child get swallowed-up by an obstructed system. She was innocent. This was an ironic injustice that happened to a good kid from a bad neighborhood.

Mrs. Closky racked her brain for a solution, "Okay, just a second. I cannot guarantee a thing, but if we enter a no-contest plea, I just may be able to persuade the court to place your daughter in the Job Corps…hopefully."

"But I have a job," Ginger interjected.

"Yours will not do, Miss Davis, the Corps involves more supervision and documentation. It is a spin-off of a program that was implemented twenty years ago in the mid-sixties. It is also experimental with limited government funds. Only a select few are considered.

Mrs. Davis felt like she was being taken on a roller coaster ride, "Where will they send my child and for how long?" Her eyes scrunched at the brow.

"Sometimes in the States, but placement is most often overseas. I cannot say where. I'm not even sure if Ginger will qualify. If she does, her record will be sealed when she turns eighteen, at which time the sentence shall terminate."

Mrs. Closky faced back at Ginger, "It will be much better than placement in a state facility where hardened young criminals exist. Shall we give it a try?" She asked.

"I don't seem to have a better choice," Ginger said, with defeat wallowing in her vocal chords.

# Chapter 5

## THE OPERATION

The Sanchez home was filled with pulsating sounds of oldies music, it flowed rhythmically from the rear of the house to the garage, where the house party filtered. People were coming from all over. Word hadn't gotten around town about the rising rate of drive-by shootings just yet. This opted for everyone to keep living freely and having fun, long after sunset, especially the Sanchez's.

They were considered to be one of the dominant families of the Mexican barrio. Because of the hierarchy, protection was abundant. Their bloodline alone was considered to be one of the deadliest to cross. Only the ill informed would plot any sort of takeover or hit on Familia de la Sanchez.

Tonight, they were in rare form. Their drunken nature and celebratory spirit enabled them to be caught with their guards down. With music at full volume, no one heard the screech of brakes from the dark sedan as it halted in front of the Sanchez's driveway. The deep-tinted windows descended. Gun aimed. A finger was steadily placed on the trigger.

Once again, a thunderous voice yelled from the sedan, "Barrio Ochentas! Eighties Rule!" Mimicking the rivals of the party-goers. The cracking sound of automatic weaponry erupted with deadly precision down the driveway and into the garage.

Part one was complete.

Throughout the city, no one or no race was safe.

The sedan was on a mission to shed blood tonight.

***

From room to room, agile bodies popped and glided along the base of the beat. Music seemed to be vibrating off the floor of this Eastside home and ringing throughout the house. The walls rattled and shook. Everyone was in sync with the flow of the atmosphere as if they were under hypnosis.

From the exterior, every motion within the house was seen through the picture window. The party seemed to be moving in silence. However, on the inside, it was quite the opposite.

The dark sedan halted, "Westside here, fools!"

Stillness engulfed the scene as they fired their weapons. Bullets crushed through the picture window in slow motion. Glass shattered. The projectiles ripped paint off the walls. Bodies fell to the floor. Deafness fell to the sound of the gun, shortly joined by a cacophony of chaos and screams.

With a double mission completed, the sedan sped off. As they drove away from the murder scene, Sergeant Burger was on a high.

"Wow! Two of these is a charge. I could do this all damn night. What about you, Faulk?"

"No freaking problem. Easy as breathing." Officer Faulk bragged.

Captain Starks was of a different temperament. Unlike his subordinates, he had bigger plans in mind and didn't find satisfaction in celebrating small victories when they were only at the start of the war.

"Our deception is due for expansion. The point of focus shall transcend from Black-on-Black assaults and Brown-on-Brown to Black-on-Brown, Brown-on-Black and any other foreign degenerates that we can intertwine."

"We'll have 'em all at each other's throat!" Officer Faulk added.

"Precisely, but balance is mandatory. They must remain pitted amongst each other as well. We don't want them too peaceful with themselves. They should never taste the power of unity!" Captain Starks yelled, grinning deviously.

"This is your captain's last mission."

A silence filled the truck.

"The two of you can function without me. I shall continue the cause from another angle. I'm due for promotion soon. Hopefully it'll be in a strategic location that will benefit us."

"We can hold down the operation," Sergeant Burger said confidently, expanding his chest. "We can't trust anyone else to assist us."

"I know. A lot of cops share our view, but few will go as far as we have," Captain Starks acknowledged.

" 'Cause they ain't got the guts!" Officer Faulk shouted.

Captain Starks sneered his lips. He knew what it really took. They were just rookies, going along for the ride in his eyes.

"I wouldn't stretch the statement that far. But you're near the mark."

# Chapter 6

## *JOB CORPS*

The top view of South Africa's landmarks, people, high-rises, and countryside amazed Ginger as she gazed outside the airplane window. She looked out to the new world she would embark on. The sun beamed mercilessly over the motherland's horizon, almost blinding her as she stared off. This was Ginger's first time on a flight, traveling all the way from the west coast. She crossed many oceans and seas to get here. The sight was breathtaking, making it all worthwhile.

*** 

Shortly after Ginger arrived, she built relationships with a few girls in the program and was finally getting adjusted.

A trim redhead, with freckles and a valley girl accent, named Robbie Russell walked down the steps of a hospital with Ginger, dressed in nurses' uniforms. They stepped into the garden area that was adjacent to the university and sat on benches to have lunch outside. This had become their daily ritual for sometime now.

"Here we dine, once again. Rather charming, isn't it?" Robbie joked using a proper voice.

"I hear you girlfriend. My uncle used to say that 'no two days were the same'." Ginger laughed, "But girl, I swear today seems like it's going to be another replay of yesterday," twirling her finger in a circular motion.

"And everyday of the past two months since we arrived here." Robbie said, plucking a rose from the bush beside her. Only moments into observing the red colored pedals, she was distracted by the sound of chanting. Her stomach dropped. Not again, she made a quick look at Ginger who sat with the same expression.

Just a distance away from where they sat, a small band of students marched to protest unequal education and apartheid at the university. They chanted and sung, "Bring Him Back Home!", an anthem for the anti-apartheid movement. Ginger and Robbie tried to drown out the noise over small talk. But after a few failed attempts, they couldn't ignore it. It wasn't much else they could do. Protests, police, and politics were the norm around this area, and they hadn't grown used to it yet. Students marching with signs, was another visual reminder to the current political state the country was in.

Back in the garden, a few of the other girls joined Ginger and Robbie. Each of them, were selected to serve as a Job Corps Nurses' Aid in South Africa for the summer. The diversity amongst this half dozen young females was undeniable. After everyone scattered about the benches and pulled out their lunches, one of the more seasoned girls decided to introduce the newbie.

"Hi…how are you, Ginger. Hi, Robbie. This is Akimi. She's from Japan. Just arrived today."

Greetings were exchanged and the girls proceeded with their meals. After a few bites into her food, Akimi decided to ask a few questions of her own.

"I come here through a foreign exchange program with my country. How about everyone else? You all be American?"

Robbie spoke up, "Ginger and myself are from California. Tina and Karen are from the Midwest. Mia and Sheila are here by way of New York…I mean New Yark."

The girls giggled at her grammar, some accents had never been heard before.

Robbie continued to make her rounds, "Pat here hails from Jamaica, the next country to be blessed with my charming presence."

"We were sent here by the courts in our country. Pat is an exchange student, like yourself." Ginger added, "and Robbie is just adventurous… She volunteered."

"I was rather incorrigible. My dad heads a big law firm. He concluded that I needed a change of scenery…and some work habits. I don't mind though. It's really rather bitching," Robbie said, rolling her eyes.

Akimi pointed a petite finger to the crowd protesting next door. She just so happened to look over when a police unit swiftly dispersing the attraction.

"What is that about?" Akimi asked with a look of concern, her finger still elevated.

"South Africa is under the apartheid system, "Karen muttered, she never knew how people would react.

Akimi's face became befuddled. She had no clue what that word meant.

Mia jumped in, "Yo!...It's like segregation was in America."

"And still is. Just ain't easy to see." Sheila said, matter-of-factly.

Ginger, shook her head, "Same effect in a more sophisticated manner. But don't trip Akimi, we'll give you a history lesson later," putting away her lunch.

Ginger felt it was only right to break it down to Akimi, just like someone had done when she first arrived. The only difference was, it was a bigger pill for Ginger to swallow.

***

That next morning, the dormitory was filled with a buzz. The majority of the girls were out of uniform and dressed in personal clothing. Their unique individuality was expressed through different styles and fashion trends, illuminating each personality. They were prepped and ready to leave for their six-hour weekend pass. Compliments were generous and their excitement was even greater.

Robbie noticed Ginger's somber state and ran over. She jumped around anxiously in front of her, "Come on Ginger, everyone is dressed. We only get these few hours on the weekend. Let's go into town, window-shop and sightsee," grabbing Ginger's arm and trying to pull her off the bed.

Ginger pulled back, "Go ahead, Robbie. I volunteered for an emergency call. Besides, I need to catch up on writing my mother. And I don't like being stopped to show my identification," speaking with a serious tone.

There were certain ramifications and extremities that came with the apartheid system. This displeased Ginger a great deal. To know that even a million miles away from home, legal systems were violent and targeted people that looked like her.

Robbie frowned and flipped a finger in the air. She could never perceive how Ginger's experience differed from hers, but she had her own reservations about the system. The shame. The demeaning and derogatory statements without filter. It disgusted her.

"Up theirs! They do it because you're Black. Once they learn who you are, they get fucking apologetic. I'm White and they ask me simply because we're together. They say it's for my protection. I get the feel of what you mean. But I still want you to come with us, please."

"They're not the only reason. If I didn't have things to do, I would go. Really I would." Ginger smiled but her mind was made up.

"I know…Oh well," Robbie extended a peace sign and hurried to catch up with the other girls.

# Chapter 7

## STUDENTS OR ASSASINS

Two Black South African Police informants sat on their knees in the middle of an abandoned shack. Their eyes were blindfolded. The rope squeezed their wrist behind their backs, causing their hands to ache. Zae Masekela, was the lookout. He guarded the door, watching the evening dust settle under a watchful eye. The two others, Malik Banda and Kumasi Kamuzu, played a different role.

They approached the informants from behind.

Malik spat between them, "You both deserve worse. But the blade is sharp." He trailed his finger along the machete, "It shall be as swift and painless as possible," encircling them.

The first informant pleaded in between sobs, "We have done nothing. Please spare our lives!" he sniffled violently.

"What is the charge against us?" the other informant asked with anger in his voice. He was a bit more bold. Unknowing his demand for answers would become his own demise.

"You know very well what the charges are!" Kumasi hissed. "Socializing , fraternizing, and collaborating with the enemy!"

Vengeance grew from the tail of his spine up his back, through his nervous system and rattled his bones. He wanted blood. Blood for his country and the betrayal of his people.

Both the captors grabbed the heads of the informants. Next, Kumasi and Malik laid them on the floor to the side. The hardened clay beneath their knees was now against their cheeks. It coldly pressed against their face and the contour of their body. They laid helplessly in a fetal position with their hands tied, eyes blinded. They could only rely on sound for any kind of perspective. This was a nightmare. Terrifying. Tortuous. A chill ran through them. They could feel the inevitable coming.

"You are traitors to your own people. You are worse than the enemy himself!" Malik circled them once more, growing into a deeper resentment.

"Please!" The informant yelled out, hunching over in full desperation. "Can we make a deal?" he asked, tears soaking through his blindfold. His sobs had grown louder. Snot hung from his nose and gravity slowly pulled it to the floor. Guilt was sinking in.

"Fire and gunpowder do not sleep together!" Kumasi commanded, with a cold mug on his face. His murderous look was unseen but they could feel his intensity all the same. They braced themselves for the worse.

Kumasi locked eyes with Malik and signaled the green light. In unison, they pierced the jugular veins and skillfully sliced the informants necks. Blood spattered against the clay. They both dropped their weapons. When the blades hit the ground beneath them, it was only sound that remained. The cries and demands stopped.

Swiftly, they slipped out of their coveralls, peeled the gloves off, and exited the sacrificial scene with caution.

\*\*\*

Zae drove the car that night with cautious eyes in the rear-view mirror. Malik and Kumasi were busy tightening their neckties and arranging clear round glasses on their faces. After they got situated, Kumasi noticed a slight change in Malik's behavior.

"Malik, why are you so quiet and distant?" He asked, concerned.

Malik lowered his eyes, "You know my feeling when we have to execute one of our own kind." The sadness in Malik's face was sadness Kumasi had also known.

"It pains me as well my brother. It is difficult but necessary."

Zae adjusted the rear-view mirror to get a better look at his friends. He wanted to commend them for their compassion, but he couldn't, not under these circumstances. He had to speak up. He couldn't drive in silence anymore.

"They aided the South African death squad! Over a dozen of our people perished by their tongues." Zae tightened his eyes and stared back at the road. "I have no remorse."

"I have none as well. I shall do it again if needed." Malik said, solemnly. "It's just difficult..." his voice faded out as he looked off to the road.

An uninvited chill crept into the car. Everyone took a moment to gather their thoughts. They seemed to be reminded of who they were and what they were doing. It affected them all in different ways.

They rode in silence for a long distance before Zae spoke again, "Who shall I drop off first?"

"It doesn't matter, I am going to the hospital to check on our soldier, Benji Jaba." Malik responded.

"Myself as well. Zae, you dispose of the car." Kumasi directed. "We shall meet at our regular time tonight."

Zae smiled, "Excellent. Give my regards to Benji with hopes of a speedy recovery."

Kumasi nodded, "Of course. It shall be done."

***

Malik and Kumasi roamed the halls of the hospital's corridor in search of Benji's room. As it got later in the evening, worry began to trickle in. They checked at least two floors and twelve rooms since they had been dropped off.

Malik was becoming angered, his patience wearing thin, "The nurse said they moved him to room 731-A. Didn't she?"

Kumasi was just as puzzled. He motioned to the sign in the hallway to get a better look, "Yes…this A-wing," placing his finger against the letter, "but no room 731."

He backed away and headed to the next room. As they walked frantically, they saw Ginger coming up the corridor, pushing a food cart. Their eyes stared her up and down as she approached.

Malik yelled, "Hey! Miss nurse…where the hell is room 731?

Ginger rolled her eyes over Malik slowly, threw her head in the air, and proceeded down the corridor without a reply.

Kumasi wasn't phased by the dramatics. They were here for a reason and she was the only one who could help them at that moment. He had to get a grip on the situation. Kumasi ran over to Ginger, so he wouldn't have to yell.

"Forgive my friend's hast little sister. We are trying to locate a sick friend. Can you please assist us?" he asked with calmness in his voice.

Ginger stopped walking. She placed an authoritative fist on her hip and sized them up. After a brief moment of hesitance, she pointed in the direction of room 731.

"Five doors down, on your right." Ginger said, blandly.

Kumasi smiled, " Thank you, Miss…ahh…" He bent over to read her nametag, "Miss Ginger Davies."

Leaning in that close changed everything. The fog cleared. It felt like a mirage was transforming in front of his eyes. Moments ago, he was so focused on his friend, Ginger appeared to be the average nurse. But his attention shifted in an instant. At this distance, he could see the depth of her attraction and how youthful she seemed to be.

"You're quite welcome. The name is Davis." Ginger corrected. "Not Davies."

She forced a smile out of courtesy and gazed over Malik with daggers in her eyes. Kumasi and Malik turned to each other, shrugged, and smiled. By this time, Ginger had already strolled down the hallway.

Malik shook his head, "A lot of fire in that one."

"Yes...I like her inner spirit. She has also been bestowed with a lot of outer beauty."

Kumasi was beyond intrigued. He made a mental note and took one final look at her before making their way over to Benji's room.

*** 

Chief Kamuzu anxiously sat in his kingly chair, stroking the gray hairs along his beard. After each stroke, he would take a deep breath to calm his impatience. The sun shined right through the windows and onto his face, this helped bring some ease. To pass the time, he would occasionally look around and observe the details of his home. He was very proud of the memories it kept. The house was built by his father years before in the center of Kwazulu Province. Since the chief took reign, he perfected the estate to his liking.

In an effort not to startle him, the housekeeper spoke at a humbled tone, "Your son awaits you in the garden, Chief Kamuzu," breaking his daze.

Chief Kamuzu snapped up, this was exactly what he was waiting for. "Thank you, Dinjah."

The chief was a robust man with dark glistening skin and oval cheeks. His majestic frame resembled that of an aged warrior. It was draped in tribal cloth as he swayed through the swinging doors. He joyfully entered the garden, at the rear of the house, and embraced Kumasi with open arms.

"Kumasi...Welcome, my son. Come...Let us walk and talk." Chief Kamuzu said, guiding him by the shoulder as they took off for a hike.

Step after step, they walked for a great distance. Their thighs tightened from the incline of the mountains and their foreheads started to sweat from the humidity. They passed so many trees along the way, they practically were in and out of the shade. Once they reached the top, they stopped at the edge of a plateau and began overlooking the cascades of Zululand. They squinted to protect themselves from the blinding sunlight. But the view was all too enticing. Their eyes daringly widened at the sight, pausing in time to enjoy the moment for a while.

"How are you studies?" Chief Kamuzu asked, breaking the silence, "And your heart…is it still filled with the desire to be a lawyer?"

Kumasi's athletic chest heaved as he took a deep breath. His high, dark cheekbones accentuated a chiseled face. His ebony eyes squinted as he peered out over Zululand. He flashed a perfect set of pearl white teeth before speaking, he knew exactly how to appease his father.

"Yes, my father, my heart is there because my heart is in our country."

"You didn't look into my eyes when you spoke. What else occupies your heart?" the chief questioned, sensing a shift in his son.

Kumasi took a few steps towards the edge, "Freedom is too slow coming. We need control of our country…now!" He turned to face his father, "White supremacy, oppression and exploitation must cease. Since sixteen fifty-two until now, has been too long."

The chief never heard such passion and intensity coming from Kumasi. But he knew Kumasi had been exposed to the ills of the country, even though they came from royal blood. The fight was unavoidable and his people had been fighting for decades.

"I am very much aware of the history of the Boers, the British, the Indians, and yes, even the division of tribes. The Afrikaners have chopped our tribal areas and consolidated them into small homelands."

The chief placed two outstretched palms on Kumasi's shoulders, his aged hands gripped tightly, "The oppression has been ongoing for hundreds of years. However, consider this, rain beats a leopard's skin…but it does not wash out the spots."

"I respect and admire your patience, my father," Kumasi smiled. "Your calmness is so natural."

"A roaring lion kills no game…Remember that," he said, looking his son directly in the eye.

"A wise man uses this," tapping his temple lightly. "That is why you must be firm with yourself. Your inclination must be restrained. You must finish school, and thus, be in a stronger position to defeat this oppression with the oppressor's own laws."

He raised his arms to the sky, "Your spirit is high like the mountain. This is good," his smile grew wide. "But it can work against you. It is the calm and silent waters that drown a man. Maintain balance, my son. A little subtly is better than a lot of force."

Kumasi reached up and lowered his father's arms, "I shall try Father."

Chief Kamuzu wrapped a weathered arm around his son, "come my son…look."

They turned about. Their eyes were welcomed to huge valleys, mountains, and pastures that encapsulated their view. It was quite panoramic. They couldn't capture the sight with just one look. The chief stepped closer to the edge of the plateau and his son followed suit.

"I give you advice and counsel…if you don't listen with more than your ears, adversity shall be your teacher." Chief Kamuzu warned. "I also want all of Azania. After our success, I would share with the Whites who have been here."

"I concur, if it is possible." Kumasi nodded.

"Nature produces many signs. In late March and late September every year, the day and night are of equal length. The light of day overcomes the dark of night and the night, in turn, revolves and gives way to light."

The chief always talked in riddles or used fables. It took Kumasi years to decode the philosophical gems his father gave him. Today was different. He understood him clearly. The challenging part came with doing the right thing and listening to his father's advice versus following his own path.

*** 

Professor Vanowen pushed up his sliding bifocals. He moved them from the tip of his hawk shaped nose and positioned them evenly at the bridge. Age-spotted fingers combed a head of white, stringy hair back into place as he concluded his morning lecture in the classroom.

"Hopefully, all of you will graduate and extend your career, in Europe or America. One day you may attain your height and head a law firm. With the extensive influx of technology on the horizon, you can implement tools to gain a competitive edge for your firm."

He sluggishly walked back and forth in front of the chalkboard, covered in legal jargon. His student body was hanging on by a thread. Some of them were slouched in their chairs and others were silently packing their items away into their book bags. Everyone knew the professor was heading toward the end of his lesson and they were about to be dismissed.

Raking his hair back once again, the professor continued his monotone delivery, "Be mindful that a processing system, for example, which can perform telecommunications functions, will enhance your services." He placed another sloth like foot in front of the other, "However, personal interaction is the key to building the relationships that assist in building a successful law firm. We shall continue tomorrow."

The classroom was brought to life. Books beat against the desk. Seats emptied. Everyone was on their feet, gathering their belongings, and filing out of the room. Malik and Kumasi were one of the first to exit and head across campus.

They passed a few fellow classmates but kept on their way. Kumasi slowed his speed as they came upon a building where no students were present.

"Malik, inform Zae of tonight's meeting. Our contact has names and locations for us."

Malik pondered to himself for a moment. He seemed unsteady. He shuffled closer to where Kumasi stood, closing the distance between them.

"My trust in our contact wavers…I often ponder his motives." Malik whispered from his lips, but his eyes screamed with suspicion.

"The issue is not color with him. The issue is freedom!" Kumasi screeched, accidently raising his tone.

Instinct set in. They paused to look around to see if anyone was approaching or listening. The coast was clear. They continued at a consistent whisper.

"He knows our true nature is peaceful and he will be able to live in harmony with us at the reins." Kumasi said.

"Hopefully so." Malik murmured ,mildly, "We shall meet tonight."

"I know. God willing, I shall see you tonight." Malik waved as he began to walk off.

"God be willing." Kumasi repeated to himself. He hurried to visit Benji again before their engagement.

***

"I expect to be out of here by next week." Benji said, laying in the hospital bed with a relaxed smile.

He was happy to finally get some company. His room had been dull up until then. His only interaction had been with nurses and a few other members of the medical staff. This was by design, due to the delicacy of their operations and oath of secrecy. It protected his brothers, but kept him in solitude during most of his recovery.

"Excellent!" Kumasi cheered excitedly, standing beside. "The cause awaits you, my brother…"

Kumasi finally felt at peace and placed a gentle hand on his friend's shoulder. They were relieved that no officials questioned Benji's accident, or tried to place him on the scene of any recent assassinations.

After a brief pause, the guys were interrupted by the sound of the door. Everything seemed to fall silent when Ginger entered the room, carrying a fresh pitcher of water. Her presence was overwhelming. It was as if she was twice her height, her energy took up the whole room.

"Good afternoon, Mr. Jabba." Ginger greeted warmly.

She had their full attention. She went to pour Benji a glass of water, her petite hand gripped the plastic handle. They observed each move. She filled the glass to the top and turned to address Kumasi. He was caught staring right back at her.

"Good afternoon, sir."

"Good afternoon, Miss Davis." Benji responded untimely, the delay was evident. He too was captivated by her beauty, but didn't intend on making it obvious.

Kumasi shifted and gestured toward the door, "Hello, Ginger."

"Oh so you remembered my first name." Ginger said, trying to keep from blushing. She was pleased.

Kumasi continued toward her slowly, "What little I observed of you boldly lingered on my mind."

"Um…whatever…I'm so sure. I come halfway around the world and hear the same script in this ear…" pointing for emphasis, "…that I heard in this one back home."

Kumasi looked at his friend with confusion. All Benji could do was shrug his shoulders and shake his head in a 'I-don't –know' fashion.

Rather than clearing the confusion, Ginger continued, "Anyway...What might your name be?"

"Kumasi Kamuzu."

Ginger frowned at the difficulty of repeating him, "Koo...What?"

Kumasi smiled, "Koo-mahhh-seee...Kamuzu."

"Prince Kumasi Kamuzu. His father is Chief Kamuzu." Benji interrupted, making his presence useful.

"Hmmm. Well, nice to meet you. I have work to do." Ginger grabbed the water pitcher and reached for the door.

Kumasi rushed over, opening the door like a gentleman, "It has been most pleasurable."

Ginger exited the room. After she walked out, Kumasi looked to Benji for affirmation, tightly gripping the doorknob in anticipation. Benji nodded in approval and that was all it took. Kumasi took off in hot pursuit of her. He passed a few rooms before catching her in the middle of the hallway.

"Will I see you tomorrow?" Kumasi asked, nearly out of breath.

Ginger played with the heir of ambiguity, "Don't know if you will or not. But I'll be here for another eight or nine months, if you care to look."

Before Kumasi could figure out exactly what she was saying, Ginger faded down the hallway and into a stairwell.

***

On the other side of the world, the cops were still on the hunt. The dark sedan's tires were peeling rubber in attempts to flee from another location. The car had disrupted the jovial camaraderie that flowed through an Asian house party. Fatal casualties were assumed to be from a rival Spanish gang.

Next, the death-aimed vehicle attacked a Brown affair. Blacks were to blame. Yet again, they fabricated another Black-on-Brown assault in South Central.

# Chapter 8

`

Kumasi approached Ginger as she sat in the garden area, taking a break.

"Hi…do you mind if I speak to you?" Kumasi asked, breaking Ginger's gaze as she looked at the flowers.

"No I don't mind." Ginger scooted over to give him some room. "Have a seat if you wish."

He graciously accepted her hospitality, angling himself directly in front of her face, "I know you are not native to South Africa. Are you American?"

"Good observation, I am not from here. I'm from California. Los Angeles to be exact."

Kumasi smiled, "Ahh. I thought so."

"You thought so, what? California or Los Angeles?"

"I felt you were from America. I did not know specifically."

She burst into laugher. Kumasi joined in. This relaxed him a bit.

He finally gathered the nerve and cleared his voice. "Ginger, is it possible that I might be able to escort you, when you have free time, to show you my country?"

"What did you say your name was?" Ginger asked. She didn't want to be rude and mispronounce it.

Kumasi pursed his lips together and spoke his name fluently, "Kumasi Kamuzu."

"Well, I just met you Kumasi, and I don't date strangers."

"It would be a safe date. Better yet, consider me your tour guide, not your date." Kumasi said sincerely, looking into her eyes.

Ginger pondered the offer, "Okay, Prince…but can I call you Kay-Kay. It's a lot easier. Or what if I call you Prince?" She asked, smiling.

"Kay-Kay will do." Kumasi couldn't stop the grin that was growing on his face. "And what can I refer to you as other than Ginger Davis?"

"My friends call me Gingee." Ginger said, proudly.

Kumasi grinned at the familiarity of her nickname, "Excellent. 'Gingee' means Ginger in some African dialects.

***

Kumasi, Zae, and Malik exited the car, stretching their legs for a moment. Their muscles were stiff from driving more than an hour from the school. Zae made sure his keys were in his pocket and led the way. They walked up a man-made pathway, toward a cottage, that was built deep in the countryside. Although the moonlight barely made its way through the trees, the three of them were all too familiar with he journey to get lost on their route in the dark of night.

When they finally reached the lantern-lit cottage, they started their usual routine. The trio grouped around Professor Vanowen as he opened an envelope, containing pictures and data on their next target. They sat in anticipation as he went through the paperwork. Tonight wasn't any different than the others.

Professor Vanowen looked down at his wooden table, smothered in confidential information. He sorted through a few pieces before picking up the main profile, "This is Captain Van Meeter, a brutal foe of equality. He owns a tavern that fronts for the Secret Society of Elimination of Blacks, Coloreds and Indians. As always, a safe and secure mission. Advance with extreme caution…He has a carnivorous cadre of bodyguards."

The professor gave each of them a serious look to reiterate his warning. The boys nodded in response. They always listened tentatively when the professor set the stage on their next case. They were in the dangerous business of taking down powerful players who supported the apartheid regime. This required a certain level of attention to detail.

Once again, they were off to the races. They studied the documents as if it encrypted a secret password. The three of them worked like a machine. Papers were passed from Kumasi to Malik and then Zae. Each played a different role. Kumasi was great with memory and strategy. Malik was more analytical and did well with research, and Zae could always connect the dots. As they worked and reviewed the case, the professor assumed his role as a humble host.

He rose to prepare something to drink. As he motioned to the stove the professor asked, "Tea anyone?"

Kumasi barely looked up to acknowledge him, "No thank you, Professor. We want to leave as soon as possible."

"Kumasi is correct, we must make haste. Is the envelope secure Zae?" Malik asked.

A stout, yet solid Zae flashed gold teeth as he parted his lips and patted himself at his waistband, "We are ready to go."

The professor stepped back to the table with an elevated teacup in his hand and began a toast, "To freedom!"

"To freedom!" the men joined.

The professor took a sip from the steaming cup, before speaking in a stern voice, "I expect to see all of you in class. Promptly with no tardiness. Our business at hand is one thing. Education is another. I will not compromise one for the other."

He took another sip and sent them off, "An old African proverb states that it is better to have an intelligent enemy, than a foolish friend. Now go."

***

The room was dim. A dozen officers sat in close quarters as they reviewed a film that showed police using whips and dogs to break up an anti-government demonstration. Everyone sat glued to the screen, analyzing events that animated across the television.

Causing an instant disruption, Commander Wolfson shouted, "Right there! Freeze the film." Everyone watched as he slowly strutted to the screen and pointed with the rod in his hand.

Without breaking his gaze, he aimed the rod at one of the faces frozen on the screen, "This is our subject. Study the black bastard." He spat. "Lock his face in your memory bank. Deposit!"

The commander turned from the screen and walked to the rear wall to click on the lights. The officers monitored his every move. He locked his eyes on the surrounding men and studied them with intensity. Everyone was fully attentive.

"Pressure from the Western world with their sanctions and such have made our leaders soft on apartheid. The troublemaker we're focused on is Sam Bluko. He has too much political attention to simply eradicate him. It must be done covertly. We will no doubt be blamed, but not seen."

He leaned his torso against the edge of the conference table and punched it repeatedly with his fist. BANG! BANG! BANG! The table rattled and shook from the impact, pencils fell to the floor. Some of the men jerked at the reaction and the others stood in anticipation of the next act.

The commander slammed both his palms on the table, "I will not- I repeat- I will not stand idle and witness the depletion and eventual destruction of a pure, White South Africa!" His voice started straining as he got more worked up.

"The order is hereby given! Destroy the target!" He yelled with exaggeration, his finger pointing to the freeze-framed face of Sam Bluko.

\*\*\*

50

Ginger and Kumasi walked along the beachfront, stopped at an Indian-owned café, and sat for lunch. After a few samosas and bites of basmati rice, Ginger's boiling curiosity forced its way to her lips.

"So tell me Kay-Kay, are you really a prince?" Ginger asked, the fantasy dazzling in her eyes.

"Yes Gingee, I am. But I do not feel special nor make a big deal of it. Perhaps I would if my people were free and independent of White bondage."

"Ummh, I see," lowering her head. She didn't know why but this saddened her. How could someone be a prince and still feel powerless? The apartheid system seemed to cast a huge weight of oppression that was felt by all classes, even students and royalty. Was it different in America? Or was it all the same? She redirected her attention back to Kumasi. For some reason, this made her feel for him all the more.

"One day, conditions will not exist as they are…One day soon."

*\*\**

The following morning, Ginger nearly jolted into tears of joy at the sight of her first bouquet of roses. They were professionally delivered to the hospital during her work hours by a messenger. She read the attached card, which simply said, "Kay-Kay."

The weeks that followed were filled with adventurous experiences across South Africa. Together, Ginger and Kumasi explored the ends and outs of the city, and the countryside. They were starting to grow on each other and shy demeanors rapidly shed. One day, they sat under a huge waterfall, engaged in play. Ginger almost slipped amongst the rocks, while Kumasi chased after her. They lost their balance when they embraced each other. The scuffs on their elbows thereafter became a running joke amongst the two.

In the beginning, Ginger tried her best to hold back, but Kumasi eventually broke her down and forced her out of her comfort zone. Ginger never felt more free than when her hair blew in the wind, as she rode bicycles alongside Kumasi, on scenic paths down the mountain. Kumasi laughed endlessly, running across flower fields and watching Ginger fall into his arms. He too was falling for her. She wasn't just the girl he fantasized about before his missions. She helped him forget all his stresses; no one had been able to do that before Ginger. Not even his father, and the comfort of his fables.

Today, the infatuation continued. Ginger and Kumasi spread a blanket on the grass and opened a picnic basket. Kumasi looked down at Ginger, as she rested in his arms. They were pretty stuffed from their goodies that were now scattered about. Kumasi didn't know what came over him but he figured he needed to say what had been pressing on his mind since the day he laid eyes on her in the hospital.

"Gingee, I must convey my true feelings for you." The words fell off his lips uncontrollably.

"And what might those feelings be?" Ginger asked, sitting up and looking back at him.

"Well…it is difficult to define what I am feeling." He could barely muster the courage to look her in the eyes, "I know it is more than a strong degree of attraction that I have acquired for you."

"We have only been knowing each other for a few months now." Ginger interrupted.

"I know," his eyes juggled between the ground and her piercing gaze. "But time has nothing to do with it. I was in love the instant I saw you." Kumasi confessed.

"Love? Don't be silly. And why should I believe you?"

"I would not lie to you."

"But still…You're not telling me why I should believe what you just said." Ginger spoke with a grade of seriousness that made Kumasi even more engaged.

"Very well, do not believe my mouth." Kumasi reached for Ginger's hands and placed them in his, "A man can make the mouth say anything."

Kumasi pulled her palms to his chest, "Man can imitate sounds of animals. A ventriloquist can throw his voice. Look into my eyes…they do not lie. Listen to my heart beating, it is the drum of my soul that thumps the truth."

Ginger looked deep into his face, with an evaluating glare. Kumasi could see she was still a bit weary, so he continued to let the words flow.

"It may take more time for you to see and hear these instruments of my inner composition that yearn to translate my true self to you."

Ginger had to admit she was captivated, but she was still vastly apprehensive. The caliber of boys who tried to talk to her, didn't have the best track record.

"Whatever. I mean it all sounds good to me Kay-Kay…but it's still just talk."

\*\*\*

"Good evening, my brethren. The night is young, but my bones are old." Sam Bluko parted from a small group of men in the township and headed toward his flat.

The men graciously added, "Be careful Sam...Look before every step."

When Sam entered his room, he shut the door and bolted it down. He felt like he was being followed. From the shade of a curtain, two gloved hands reached up to Sam's back. Swiftly, a metal wire slipped around his neck. Sam's hands clawed at the wire in a fruitless attempt to release it. His body slowly slid down to death.

***

Kumasi and Chief Kamuzu walked along a mountainside in the Zululands. The weight of these walks seemed to increase with time. They also became more frequent as Kumasi uncovered new chapters of his manhood. Each carried a different story, ask, or decision in need of his father's guidance.

"The most beautiful fig may contain a worm, my son."

"No Father...She is beautiful inside and outside as well," Kumasi exclaimed, hoping his objection didn't seem dishonorable. He respected his father. But with Ginger, the king's fables didn't stand up against his love for her.

The chief turned to his son, "You know how strongly I follow our customs. But if you are certain her heart shines as brightly as her teeth, I shall give my blessings to your marriage. Of course, I must meet her first. And I pray that union will not interfere with your education."

Kumasi was ear to ear, this is exactly what he wanted to hear. "Thank you, my father. I do not know when because I have yet to ask her. I had to seek your approval before I gave the thought further consideration."

The chief nodded with a smile and they continued to walk. Kumasi's double life was moving fast but everything was falling into place.

\*\*\*

At the university, Professor Vanowen leaned back in his desk chair, faintly smiling. He read the newspaper headlines that announced the car bomb assassination of Captain Van Meeter. With a sinister look, he thought silently to himself, job well done.

\*\*\*

Less than twenty-four hours later, Ginger and Kumasi strolled along the ocean shoreline. Waves pushed up against their ankles as the tide began to rise.

"Listen, Kay-Kay." Ginger said sharply, getting his attention. Her toes nervously gripped the damp sand beneath them.

"I will be going back home real soon and we don't need to do anything except enjoy the here and now. I am young and haven't even experienced a serious relationship. I don't need a heartache. Love ain't on the menu. Yes, you have turned an adverse situation in my life into the most exciting and fulfilling time that I have ever experienced. I have never been this happy. But I must return home. Boy, you must be tripping…You don't want to marry me!"

Her voice seemed to echo along the sea. A pause lingered and Ginger looked away. Her foreign fantasy was coming to a close. The pure thought of home caused reality to sink in like a battered ship. Kumasi brought something different out of her. Something she hadn't experienced in California, for all those years. She felt free. A sense of peace and protection. And although the entire ordeal felt surreal, what Kumasi just offered took her over the top. Her mind flooded with thoughts as she observed where the ocean met the sky. A world of disbelief seemed to be resting on her shoulders.

"Yes I do," Kumasi spoke passionately, with a penetrating stare.

Ginger sighed with exhaustion, "I'm sorry, I must unite with my mother."

"I can send for your mother."

Ginger couldn't help but laugh. Mrs. Davis was a true California girl. She couldn't picture her mother in South Africa, a million miles away from her comfort zone.

"I want her out of the projects…but ain't no way she'll come here. No kind of way."

"Will you please consider my proposal?"

"Okay, I will. But I'm sure I won't change my mind."

Ginger glanced back to the open sea, crossed her arms and thought about the possibilities. She couldn't believe this was all happening. Some part of her didn't want to trust it. She didn't know what it was. It wasn't that he seemed untrustworthy, but there seemed to be a shadow that had yet to come to the light.

# Chapter 9

## HOLLYWOOD HILLS

Captain John Starks, Sergeant Burger, and Officer Faulk met in a highly secluded area of the Hollywood Hills. Meetings and debriefings occurred here since they began their operation. It was a distance away from any nearby neighborhoods and covered in California's finest palm trees and bushes. The perfect disguise. They easily hid themselves and their parked squad cars with the help of Mother Nature. They favored this location and cherished it like a corner office.

Officer Faulk sat on a tree stump while Sergeant Burger took a smoke break. As time passed, Officer Falk drifted off into a daydream. His eyes traced over the Los Angeles skyline, when something told him to look over his shoulder. He instantly nudged Sergeant Burger who disposed of his cigarette when he too noticed the captain quickly approaching.

The captain cut to the chase and began talking while he walked up, "Gentlemen...I called this meeting to inform you that we must defer our assignments."

"Awhh, Captain, you gotta be shitting us!" Officer Faulk huffed.

"Calm down, Faulk…let me continue." Captain Starks said, positioning himself inches away from them.

His body language juxtaposed their tense muscles and worried eyes. Sergeant Burger and Officer Faulk hung onto their captain's next words like fish on a hook. They anticipated what his guidance would entail. Their attention was unwavering.

"The deferment shall be temporary. You don't fully understand the dynamics of our scheme. I do, and I know what is best."

He was right. Sergeant Burger and Officer Faulk didn't know they were solely on the frontlines of a broader, more political agenda. Captain Starks led the efforts from their side, but he too, only operated by what he was told. He thought it would be best to keep them in the dark, only giving them pieces of the puzzle.

"How long before we continue, Captain?" Sergeant Burger asked.

"You'll be informed of the re-engagement date, Sergeant. It is merely a precautionary move." He held up his pointer finger, "Deception is one of our pillars."

"Well, I hope it ain't long," Officer Faulk said, souring his face. "I look forward to our missions, " dropping his head.

He was anxious and wanted to continue the dirty work. This entire ordeal annoyed him. Repression added weight to his depression. Being contained was like a death sentence for Officer Faulk. He harvested post-traumatic stress from boarding schools and a militant family. This drove him to the police force in the first place. He wanted to be on the other side of the law and control cages versus being thrown in another one.

"Me too. I'm hooked." Sergeant Burger agreed, smiling like a mischievous toddler.

Captain Starks placed his hand on the sergeant's shoulder. His stature seemed to be larger than life, standing well over six feet. The dominating presence and level of seniority made him come off like a tyrant.

He gripped with authority, "That's exactly why we need to check and evaluate our position. I'll give you the command in due time. I project it to be in a month or two, so carry on in regular fashion."

"We read you, Captain. Whenever you send the order, we'll be ready." Officer Faulk looked him directly in he eye.

Captain Starks withdrew from their circle and walked to his jeep. He grabbed an automatic weapon out the truck, aimed, and unleashed multiple rounds at a target on the mountainside. He had an AK and returned the smoking weapon back to the rear of the jeep. The weight of the gun thumped against the trunks metal.

Another benefit to the hills was the sound barrier; nothing could get between the mountains. Gunshots could not be heard from way up here. Even though the officers knew this, the captain's behavior still caught them off guard. They slowly walked toward him with wide eyes.

Captain Starks took a deep breath, "That felt good gentlemen. I trust you shall adhere to practice in absence of assignments. I will feed you names of suspects from my office. They will be the ones we cannot make a case on. But you will. Check the central file. Tail them. When you stop them, they will have dope or weapons in their possessions, won't they?"

"Of course." Officer Faulk exclaimed.

"Oh, yeah. I copy," Sergeant Burger added.

Captain Starks checked his watch, "I have a meeting to attend. The chief wants me to spearhead a new program for victims of a gang violence."

Strangely, he burst into laughter and stared into the sky with a diabolical grin, "I have stepped into the shadows. But I am sure it will be to our advantage in the long run. The White race is depending on us."

"Damn right they are!" Officer Faulk yelled.

"Many Whites would oppose our method of operandi." Captain Starks spoke solemnly, "But they'll be grateful in the end."

# Chapter 10

## THE PROPOSAL

Ginger, Robbie, Mia and Karen sat in the dormitory quarters engaged in their daily chitchat. Some laid on the floor, others hung off the bed and played with pillows. All the while, Ginger had the stage.

"And then he spills this elaborate proposal all over me." Her hands stretched open, bright eyes bulged and her face filled with shock. She was fully animated in her expressions, and the girls loved every bit of it.

"Girl...no he didn't." Mia smirked, sitting Indian-style. Ginger gave her a 'would-I –lie-to you' look and rolled her eyes.

Robbie jumped in, full of excitement, "Wow! That's fuckin' far out. It's so very intriguing. Go for it, Gingee. You'll be a princess." She pretended to put on a crown. Everyone pointed and laughed, except for Mia. She wasn't easily convinced and decided to voice her opinion once again.

"Robbie...homeboy just talking. We done heard it all in the hood, I mean every syllable."

Their stale faces encouraged Mia to continue, "And you know that's right! Dreams are sold every minute of a day. And yo, guess who does the paying?" she asked. No one responded. It was obvious she thought this sounded like one big fairytale. But some of the other girls were a bit more optimistic.

Robbie sat up and leaned in closer. She began to break down the options for Ginger, "Let us say, he's for real…" She raised her right hand, "If it doesn't work out, you have youth on your side; it's not like you won't get another proposal in life. If it does," she raised her left hand, "you'll live happily ever after with a lot of awesome adventures in between."

Karen broke into laughter, "Yeah, right. It sounds like something straight out of a story book."

They all cracked up laughing. Ginger only giggled for a moment. Something was weighing on her. Perhaps, it was the hope that for once she could have something great, without fighting for it. The tables had turned. Kumasi was fighting for her. She liked being on this side of the ring, but she was still confused all the same.

"It's all so very amazing to me. I really do have feelings for him and I keep sensing that he really means what he says."

Mia had heard enough. She wasn't having it, "Yo, Gingee, I'm telling you, in South Central or South Africa, bullshit is bullshit," giving a dismissive wave of the hand.

Ginger shrugged. Aside from this fantasy, she was facing a pressing timeline.

"Oh well, whatever. My term will be up in a few months and I plan on returning home. That's foremost in my mind.... But I just don't know for sure."

"I heard that." Mia hyped. "I'll be so glad to get back to the asphalt jungle that I don't know what to do! And I'm for sho."

Ginger let out a sigh of relief and turned back to Robbie, "What about you Robbie? What are your plans? We leave around the same time."

Robbie started dancing reggae style, "Well ladies, Robbie Russell shall be sighted on the sands of Jamaica, basking in the sun with some lucky young surfer rubbing my body down with exotic oils," swaying her hips. "Pat has run it all down to me. Now all a girl has to do is convince my dad that I've been good and need a debriefing, stress-free vacation in my life."

Karen smiled, "I hope you make it and may all of your dreams come true."

"I hope so too. You deserve it. You're the coolest White girl I ever met." Mia added.

Robbie playfully wiped her eyes, "Awhh, quit it before I get all fuckin' mushy." They all laughed in response.

Unlike some of their hometowns and the apartheid system, within their small circle they experienced friendship and sisterhood without racial, political or social barriers. The purity was unique. It taught them all something different. Their girl talks brought them closer; it was meditation for some and a ritual for others.

Robbie put all jokes aside and placed a comforting hand on top of Ginger's knee, "I'm sure that whatever you decide to do, we're with you. If you decide to go home, I'll leave my dad's number and address to his law firm. If you ever need a job, he will see to it that a position is developed for you, just tell him that you were here with his daughter, Robbie. I'll call him tonight and follow up when we leave."

"I'll definitely need a job. Thank you, Robbie."

Robbie gave a nod of acknowledgement. And just like that, the chitchat was adjourned. They all rose from their seats, reached for their uniforms and prepared for work.

\*\*\*

Kumasi decided to expose Ginger to different cultural experiences throughout the city. He figured, if he showed her beauty in the music, aromas, and people, she would fall deeper in love with him and the land. Only then, would she choose to stay.

Luckily, the South African city was filled with historic tribal influences and modern colonial developments – they explored it all. As a treat to the desirous-eye, the two went window-shopping in downtown Johannesburg. Kumasi then escorted Ginger to an African festival. It was filled with beating drums and shirtless women who covered themselves in beaded jewels for the celebration.

The base of the drums seemed to move through Ginger, placing her in a trance. She was overtaken by nostalgia. The beating drums synced with her beating heart. The women grabbed her hands and brought her into the circle. It felt like the entire village was connected through her palms. It was an energy she couldn't describe - A sense of unity that expanded from an atom, to the universe, and through the people. She enjoyed every bit of it. Kumasi later explained that they performed this custom for centuries to strengthen the tribe and welcome good spirits.

Later that day, Ginger and Kumasi walked across a bridge in the middle of the park. Kumasi stopped and faced Ginger with firmness in his eyes, "Your departure date is very near at hand. I must know one way or another. Have you decided?"

Ginger smirked, "You're not very observant!"

"Quite the contrary. What do you mean?" Kumasi wasn't catching on.

"You need to look into my eyes and listen to my heartbeat." Ginger uttered in a sultry voice with a welcoming smile.

Kumasi was overwhelmed. It was clear now. He reached for her waist and pulled her in close. They instantly embraced and kissed passionately, melting into one figure as they faded.

*** 

Karen, Mia, Robbie, Pat, Tina, Sheila and Akimi surrounded Ginger. Each of them made sure her traditional dress fit properly and every hair was patted into place. They were huddled in one of the large rooms of the guesthouse at Chief Kamuzu's mansion. The wedding would take place on his estate; this was a tradition that had been passed down in their tribe for ages. It signified strength of the family lineage. Ginger would fall in line with brides and princesses before her time.

Sheila marveled over the stitching and embroidery of Ginger's gown, "Your dress and jewelry are divine. And you are so beautiful. Forgive me if I cry. Funerals and weddings have an effect on me," dabbing at a tear rolling out the corner of one eye, "I'm just happy for you."

Mia handed her a tissue, "Yo' Sheila, why you gotta be so damn sentimental? This is a wedding, not a funeral. You be trippin'."

Ginger reached around and rubbed her back, "It's alright, Mia. I feel like crying myself 'cause I'm scared. But, I also feel joyous. Am I losing it, or what?"

Ginger wasn't like most brides who dreamt of their wedding and planned every detail to the tee. The only thing she ever expected was her mother's presence. But, not today. Everything was different.

Reality sank deeper and deeper as she looked at the surrounding faces. Just months ago, they had been strangers and now they were family. Their collective feminine energy would fill the void of her mother.

Even her dress was different. It wasn't the traditional white worn by Western brides. This dress was colorful and bold; it would make a rainbow envious.

Robbie looked at everyone through the mirror, adjusting herself to perfection, "It's all relative. Your mom cried on the phone also, remember?"

"Yeah, she did." Ginger smiled, "She got better when I told her Kumasi would send me home in a few months. I hope I can persuade her to return with me."

Pat was listening to every word as she strapped up her shoes. When she finished, she walked over to Ginger, "Don't worry…in time, everything will work out."

"I know it will, that's why I decided to follow my heart and deal with whatever comes later."

They looked on with admirable eyes and nodded their heads in approval. A few loving hugs spread around the group. It was almost time. They each took one final peek at their reflection and filed out of the room. Their dresses blossomed and swayed with the wind as they walked into a long corridor that led to the outside grounds.

Thousands of people engaged in joyful festivities to celebrate the marriage that took place. The lawn area was filled with song and traditional dance. Food and drinks were abundant. Joy and laughter overflowed the atmosphere. At dusk, the shadows of Kumasi and Ginger were seen sneaking away from the guest in front of a huge amber sunset backdrop. The wedding had come to a close but their lives together had just begun.

They were over the broom and swept into bed. Ginger took in a deep breath and let out with a sigh, "I'm a virgin Kay-Kay and I hope I don't disappoint you."

With a smile he spoke, "Eve probably felt the same way with Adam, just relax and let things happen naturally."

A passionate kiss lit the fire…a warm tongue manifested a purr and juices began to flow like a raging river. Slowly and deeply he thrust his manhood into her…his girth filled her garden to the very roots of delight. Ginger screamed spasmodically!...Skyrockets were shooting throughout her body. But she couldn't move. Hanging on a cliff of climax Kay-Kay's grip slipped across the moon side of Ginger's sweaty hips. Ginger's insides were tumbling in wonderland…their bodies flinched in tremors. Her legs couldn't stop shaking as they exploded together in perfect unison. Deep into the night the sound of pleasure repeatedly shot thru the village, followed by whispers of ecstasy whistling thru the trees.

# Chapter 11

## *DOUBLE, TRIPLE LIVES*

Ginger was carefully preparing breakfast in their apartment when Kumasi entered the kitchen and delivered a surprising kiss on her jaw. She jumped back in a brief moment of surprise, but smiled when she realized who it was. Kumasi took a seat at the table, all the while keeping his eyes on his wife.

"Your breakfast will be ready in about five minutes." Ginger said as she lifted a pot of smothered potatoes and eggs from the stove with an oven mitt, swatting the steam away from her face. Ginger had grown to love cooking since they moved in together, her mother prepared all of their meals back home. She was happy to cook for someone for a change instead of the other way around.

Kumasi sat back, "That will be perfect, Gingee…my first class starts in an hour." He glanced up at the clock and drifted into deep thought. Something was on his mind.

After a pause he broke his silence, "I want you to meet me at noontime today." He nervously fumbled with his fingers, "I have something of grave importance to share with you."

Ginger reached into a cabinet and pulled down a couple plates, "If it's that important, maybe you should tell me now." She turned to him with plates in hand and curiosity smeared across her face.

Kumasi whispered, "No, dear. The walls are often laced with ears," looking out the corner of his eye.

Ginger stood back in confusion, "Come on, Kay-Kay, what's going on…I hate suspense. And I told you, I ain't going for none of that spooky stuff."

Kumasi relaxed himself to bring her some ease. "Don't worry. It is not what you think I will be in the park at noon."

He shined his pearly whites against his deep melanin and motioned towards her. She openly obliged. His charisma worked every time.

\*\*\*

The time had come. Kumasi had to follow through with his promise. The location was strategic. He hoped the park's serenity, at high noon, would keep them calm for what he was about to reveal.

"Please forgive me for not informing you of what I am about to tell you." Kumasi grabbed Ginger hands as they sat on a bench facing a family of trees.

Ginger looked with anxiety. But Kumasi had to push through the uncertainties. Ginger was his wife and she deserved to know the truth.

Kumasi became anxious too. He gently squeezed her hands and cleared his throat, "You have been here a little over a year and I know you have noticed the social conditions that exist in this country."

Ginger titled her head to the side, "Of course I'm aware. I've had the displeasures of first-hand experience."

"Very well…but allow me to continue." Kumasi pulled himself closer, "On the surface apartheid is cruel, unusual and unjust punishment. But what you do not see are the vicious acts of hatred that lurk under the shade of night. A white hit-squad maneuvers under the disguise of police and other officials. Anyone who does not possess deaf ears, blind eyes and a silent tongue to apartheid is a threat to them. They are targeted and eliminated by brutal force."

Ginger opened her mouth in shock, "I didn't know. But now, I understand." She regained her composure, "What I don't understand is where you fit in."

Kumasi hesitated, "Well…" He struggled with his words, "What I am trying to convey is that Malik, Zae, Benji and myself are opponents of apartheid…all phases of apartheid."

Bewilderment lingered on her expression, "You have never displayed any open resistance to apartheid." Ginger couldn't believe what she was hearing. "All of you are law students. You, and them as well, are very studious looking…you don't participate in any rallies or demonstrations. Now, I'm really in the dark."

She stood up and placed her hands on her hips. In her mind, rebels and students followed different paths. They looked different. Talked. Walked. Dressed. And most importantly, carried themselves differently. Ginger was caught between her thoughts and fears all over again. It wasn't her future she worried about, it was his.

Kumasi could feel the tension. He had to come clean. This was the only way it would all make sense. It was the right thing to do. And his conscience was eating at him. Telling Ginger would free her from the lies and the cover-ups. And it would free Kumasi from the pressing guilt.

Kumasi gathered himself and prepared for the worse, "No, we do not exhibit any displeasure whatsoever, not openly." He braced himself for the storm, "the truth is we counteract apartheid at night. We are one of a few secret squads that eradicate the advocates of social injustice by all means necessary."

Before he could finish, Ginger's mouth was frozen in a dropped position. Her eyes and ears were wide open. She staggered back to the bench as if she were in a daze. The truth had blown her mind. She buried her face into her hands to cope.

"I should have told you before now," Kumasi pleaded. His timing couldn't have been more perfect. They were well into their marriage before he made the decision to tell her. "I take full responsibility for my error and shall honorably accept any repercussions that may result."

Ginger snapped, "Damn right you should have told me. Don't hide anything from me. Give me the choice to decide if I want to put up with a certain situation or not."

She was no longer shocked, but angry, "Kay-Kay, how could you? You do the same things that the people do who oppress you. How can it be right?"

"I am sorry. Can you forgive me?"

"I want you to quit!" Ginger screamed, fervently.

Kumasi had never seen her so worked up but she had good reason to be. And he had good reason to do what he did for his people.

"I know I am committed to you. But the commitment to my country began hundreds of years ago. I cannot quit until apartheid quits."

"The approach you use is wrong. I can't help but to say it as I feel it is. I love you, Kay-Kay, please attack them in a more peaceful manner."

Passion overwhelmed him. He didn't believe in peace when it came down to his people and the violent acts that had been bestowed upon them for centuries. Kumasi shook his head and stood up.

"It would render no effect. They respect violence...not talk."

She couldn't take it anymore. Ginger depleted all the resistance in her body with one huge exhale. She slumped over as her bones weakened. Kumasi scooped her up and supported her knees with robust arms that caressed her tenderly.

The last thing Kumasi wanted was an ultimatum. It was a battle he could not win. But he knew the weight of the situation and how the truth could change things.

He spoke faintly in her ear as she laid in his arms, "I shall force myself to understand if you decide to sever our union."

Ginger violently turned to him with sharp words, "Don't put stupid suggestions in my head...I just might follow them!"

72

She pulled herself away from Kumasi, "I haven't been living life for a long time but I ain't never quit or given up on anything. The deception you put on me is grounds to leave, but I made my commitment to God, you and myself as well. I'm not saying I won't leave you, because I will!"

Ginger was now on her feet, "But I won't until I try to make it work. I don't owe that to you…I owe it to myself! All I can say at this point is to please be careful. You have a child coming and he or she will need…"

A what? A CHILD! Kumasi rushed up to her in an exhilarating state of surprise. "Ginger! Did I hear you correctly?" He asked, with much excitement in his voice.

Ginger reached down and held her stomach, flat in shape but filled with life, "You're going to be a daddy. Will that alter your convictions?" she asked, matter-of-factly.

`Kumasi paused for a long time, looking back hundreds of years. When he finally spoke, it was very soft and his voice seemed to drift off, "I hope not."

Ginger shook her head, "You are one stubborn man."

***

While Ginger took up a new life in South Africa, her mother was back at home living a life of solitude. Aside from her coworkers and neighbors, she barely had any interaction at all. To cope, she followed a rigorous daily routine. It was built subconsciously to distract her from missing and worrying about her daughter. But what was a mother to do?

Some nights, she would reason with herself and consider that at Ginger's age, she was bound to leave home for college or other opportunities. Other nights were different. She would be in total disbelief and prepare an extra plate of food, just in case Ginger decided to pop up or surprise her.

Mrs. Davis started cooking one night when she was interrupted by the doorbell. She walked out of the kitchen and headed towards the front door of her apartment. This might be the night!? She rarely had any visitors these days so she could only hope for the best. When she opened the door, she was surprised to be greeted by Big Tasha.

"Good afternoon Mrs. Davis."

Mrs. Davis gently opened the door, "Hi Tasha...come on in," gesturing for her to enter. "How are you and how about your mother? I been missing her at church, is she alright?"

Big Tasha walked in with ease, happy she found her at the right time, "I'm fine Mrs. Davis. Momma's alright too. Her pressure has been up and she was on the tired side. How's Gingee doing? Ain't she 'bout ready to come home?"

"Child, come take a seat," fluffing a few pillows on the couch. "Let me tell you something. You hungry? Or want something to drink?" Mrs. Davis asked, walking back towards the kitchen. Her spirits slowly brightened and the smile that was once distant, returned. Although Big Tasha wasn't Ginger, she was her closest friend, and that was good enough for Mrs. Davis, for the time being.

"No thank you, Momma...I'm straight." Big Tasha said, sitting down on the couch. Mrs. Davis joined her. Big Tasha could barely keep still as the concern for her friend mounted, she was anxious to hear the news.

"Is Gingee alright?"

"I pray so. She done up'ed and married one of them Africans over there where she's at. Lawd, I hope he's a good man," biting her lip.

Married? Big Tasha was taken aback. As long as she had known Ginger, Ginger never mentioned boyfriends, let alone a husband. She couldn't even recall if Ginger had a few crushes growing up. But maybe that was just it... Ginger had grown up.

"Say what!...Gingee is married. Wait till the homies hear this. Is she coming back home with him?"

It was such a weighted question that Mrs. Davis slid her forefingers up and down the side of her temple. She then closed her eyes from what felt like barbells resting on her lids and clenched her jaw, "Say that Africa is her home...but she will come and visit regularly. I sho' prays so, 'cause as bad as I want to be with my baby, I ain't going to no Africa."

"Why not, Mrs. Davis? They say that's the O.G. homeland." Big Tasha kidded.

"Humph...I was born right here in these United States," pointing to the ground beneath her. "If the Lawd wanted me there I would've been born there."

"I hear that," Big Tasha couldn't help but laugh. "But I wouldn't mind checking the set out over there, you know what I'm saying...kinda like a vacation for a minute or so."

"Well I tell you Tasha, Gingee and her husband have made plans. I hope she finds happiness and I hope we can somehow be more close to one another. I mean the distance and all."

Mrs. Davis rocked in her seat, "But plan they may…I know that the Lawd is the Master Planner. His plan is the best of plans, so I ain't worried. No, I worries not. I just continues to pray and leave things in God's hands." She clasped her palms together in the posture of prayer.

Mrs. Davis was always spiritual but with Ginger's absence, she grew deeper into the religion. Unbeknownst to her, she was masking her fears with theological influences.

Tasha grinned at her optimism. This helped Big Tasha with the longing she felt since Ginger left. If her own mother could be content, so could she. After a nod of approval, she rose to her feet, "We'll see what's up. Give Gingee my greetin's of love and respect."

***

Ginger's belly had grown relatively large. At a projected six-months of pregnancy, there was a cantaloupe-sized stomach that carried her unborn child. The more the child grew, the disputes between the parents increased.

Ginger stood between the doorway of their bedroom and watched Kumasi as he gathered his gear to leave on another assignment. She was overcome with hormones and concern, a lethal combination. Her intuition was boiling with uncertainty. She battled with it throughout the previous night. She pleaded with Kumasi and tugged on his arm as he walked past her into the living room.

"Please don't go, Kay-Kay. You have no idea how much I worry when you leave at night. Something is wrong. I can't touch it…but I feel it."

Kumasi tried to calm her nerves, "You always tell me not to go. You always worry. But Kumasi always comes home," he said strongly, grabbing hold of both her hands.

His lifestyle triggered many fights since the day at the park and he had grown used to it because there was no way around it. He had to do what he had to do. He knew she would be right there and he would be all right. Today wasn't any different than the rest. It had become a bit of a routine.

He hurriedly rushed to the door with gear in hand, "Try not to worry. I shall return shortly. Now, I must go…everyone is waiting."

He didn't want to see her like this, but he didn't want to be late either. Tonight was big. The team had a high priority assignment. One that involved those linked to Sam Bluko's murder. It was essential that the mission was seamless. People were growing in outrage from the political assassination of their leader – something had to be done. There was talk that someone new would be appointed. A few days ago, the professor sat him down personally to tell him that their small unit would be up for consideration and he was keeping a keen eye on him. His influence over the Zulu kingdom was ideal to keep the rally going. He hadn't told his partners nor Ginger about any of this. He was balancing a lot.

Recently, the guys complained about his level of focus and dedication to the mission. Before Ginger came into his life, Kumasi was hard wired with school and secret assignments. He lived, breathed, and ate with a mission. But with his wife and growing family, he seemed to be living in three worlds. Two he could manage, but the third was wearing down on him. This was too much for any one man, even a multi-faceted beast like Kumasi.

Each life required a different characteristic and aspect of his personality. But how can one be a fighter and come home to be a lover? How could he leave schoolbooks in his backpack, only to load another bag filled with weapons? How could he kiss his wife with the same lips he cursed people with before killing them? How could he be intimate with Ginger and intimidate the enemy? It was only the conviction in himself and his beliefs that kept him grounded. Failure to him was incredulous. Alike his body, he had an even stronger mind. Nothing would keep him from becoming a lawyer, keeping Ginger or counteracting apartheid.

He couldn't let them wait any longer. Kumasi reached out and grabbed for Ginger, his hand clinging to the doorknob. He rubbed his unborn child and kissed his wife before slowly letting go. Kumasi gave her an 'I'll-be-ok-just-trust-me' look and left out the door. He walked down the back steps where his companions awaited him.

Ginger returned to the sink to wash dishes but she felt something move in the pit of her stomach, and it wasn't the baby. There was a sudden screech of brakes outside. The sound caused her to drop a plate on the floor. Glass shattered against the ground. She screamed Kumasi's name as spontaneous shots rang out. Immediately, Ginger saw another whirling repetition of the captain's face, the dark sedan, the other officers, and flashes of the drive-by at home. Pain engulfed her in the moment. She stood at the sink, dazed and confused. Glass at her feet. Mouth hung wide. Bullets flying past her.

When she finally gained the strength, she checked her body for any signs that she or the baby had been harmed. She realized she was ok and headed to face her worse nightmare. When she opened the door, Kumasi and three soldiers of freedom were lifelessly sprawled out on the ground. Their limp bodies soaked in their own blood. They were now martyrs for their country, their people. Just like that, Kumasi's triple life ended.

***

Later that afternoon, a tear-filled Ginger walked hand-in-hand with Chief Kamuzu in the heart of Zululand along the garden. Ginger tried to find security in the chief's words. But inevitably, she knew that even in his best attempt, whatever he said could not heal her fresh wounds. She was cut too deep.

"We were only married seven months ago, Chief. Why were we ripped apart? Why was our life together so short?" Ginger questioned, sobbing uncontrollably.

Chief Kamuzu tried to console her, "Your short chapter together was written long before you and Kumasi met, my child. It was penned by a much higher source. A source whose knowledge is far superior to ours. I do not know why…some things in life are far beyond our capability to understand.

The chief cleared the lump in his throat and gathered himself, he too was in mourning. He chose his next words carefully.

"Kumasi's spirit lives. I must be content with that, or wander like a rabid dog."

"You are right and I know it. The trauma is just so devastating. One part of me says life must go on, the other says it's all over." Ginger confessed.

"Everyone shall taste death, there are no exceptions, it demolishes the body but it is to the spirit as rain is to a barren plot of land. You are very strong and very brave, my daughter. You shall overcome the pain. When the skin is cut it heals and becomes tougher."

"Thank you, Chief…thank you for the encouraging compliment. I hope that in time I'll overcome the weakness I feel when I close my eyes and see Kumasi's face."

"You shall see his face again." Chief Kamuzu smiled.

Ginger forced one in return, "I know. I am full with his child, yet I feel so empty."

"Do not worry. As the child grows, it shall fill the void."

They turned around and headed back to the chief's home. Ginger looked to him, "Thank you, Father. I am suddenly a lot better. A whole lot better than I was before we talked."

Chief Kamuzu welcomed a slow grin, "This is good."

As they walked, Ginger silently collected her thoughts. There was a gripping question she was grappling with. Midway on the path, she froze in her tracks in front of a sea of white and yellow Arum Lilies. It was as if something came over her.

"I want to have my baby here so that you can share Kumasi's extended life, but I also want to go home. What should I do?"

The chief gazed up into the sky and pointed with an old, yet wise finger, "Follow the sun…it sets in the West. Go home, my child. My grandson shall automatically be a citizen and heir of Zululand by blood. He can always rise and return to the East. If he is born in your America, he will also be a citizen there. Both are better."

"You are very kind and unselfish."

Ginger looked down at her stomach. She sent a silent prayer that her seed would carry genes from Kumasi and the chief – a grave sense of morality and humility.

"It is like the deep thrust of a long spear. It pains me deeply because the child will not be raised by the whole village," the chief said, extending his arms wide. "Nonetheless, I know it is best for you to go home and return some other spring."

Ginger hugged him. Damp with tears, she choked at her words, "I'm sorry. The tears are tears of happiness. You have paved a way for me. I think I can make it now."

Chief Kamuzu spoke at a tone that sounded more like a hum. He was very subtle in his delivery, "I understand the tears. If my river were not drying up, I would have enough to flow on the outside."

She lifted from the tips of her toes and served the chief with a heartfelt kiss on the cheek, "Thank you again, Chief. I will faithfully send photos and letters until our return." Ginger said joyously.

With a humble voice the chief uttered, "May the peace and blesssings of the Creator forever be upon you and ours. May you both grow strong and one day be guided back home, my princess."

# Chapter 12

## THE RETURN

Through Ginger's earphones, she bobbed her head to the beat as she looked down on the city of Los Angeles from an aerial view. She listened to the music as her passenger jet descended and landed at LAX. The next thing she knew, she was already in the taxi and in route to her old neighborhood. It was all too hazy for her. Everything was moving fast.

While in the midst of her thoughts, Ginger's expressionless face was caught in the mirror by the taxi driver. He stared periodically while gnawing on a wet cigar nub. After a long silence, he spoke out of one corner of his mouth while the other side steadily balanced the tobacco.

"I see you're in a motherly way," he said, holding his glance in the rear view, "I'll go ahead and take you beyond the bus stop. I don't normally go into any of the projects…guess I can bend the rules this one time."

His offer was generous but Ginger was barely paying attention. "Thank you. I'm tired…" She met his eyes in the mirror but looked away quickly after, "It's been a long journey."

"Where you coming from?" The driver asked, persistent to spark up a conversation.

Ginger pondered the question until she had something to say, "A swift life that seems like a bad dream," giving the best answer she could think of.

The driver peeked into the mirror once again. He noticed something deeper seemed to be bothering her and decided to proceed in silence for the rest of the drive. In his line of work, he would catch people on their best and worse day. It was a spectrum. You never knew the path someone was on when you encountered them.

Ginger and the driver finally arrived to the projects after they took a huge detour to avoid Los Angeles's infamous traffic. As they pulled up, she glanced over the building from the car and sat still for a moment. Everything looked the same, but it all seemed drastically different. When she finally picked up the courage to get out of the car, she did so slowly. Emotional weight and pregnancy were to blame.

When she reached her mother's apartment, her face was full of shock as the door opened. It seemed like thousands of people were gazing back at her. Shouts of 'SURPRISE' rang in her ears, the smell of home cooked food graced her nose, and her eyes were filled with faces from a familiar life she once lived.

Ginger absorbed the abundance of hugs and kisses while staggering through the apartment. From the front door, she could see flying banners in the backyard. When she got a little closer, she saw that the banners read, "Welcome Home Ginger", announcing her homecoming. As she reached the patio area in the backyard, she realized that it was packed with people from the neighborhood. Everyone was filled with joy when they saw her. Their Gingee had finally returned. The music erupted and a party jumped into full effect.

There was a dominoes table, a group of people playing spades, and someone was always on the dance floor. It was a true community gathering action. The older women helped prepare the food and the men watched over the grill like hawks. There was no burger or rib untouched by the grace of their hands.

Later into the festivities, Ginger was surrounded by a flock of girls who had endless questions about her journey. Their beaming eyes and thirsty ears awaited her story like a child during bedtime. Each of them were from the projects and had never stepped foot outside of Los Angeles.

Big Tasha returned to the group after grabbing her second appetizer plate, "You ain't missed a damn thing, home girl. Same circus, different clowns," she said, matter-of-factly and flopped into her seat.

"And you know that's right!" One of the homegirls added.

Ginger looked around at the people dancing, singing, and eating. She couldn't believe she was all the way back on the West Coast. She had returned to the nest and felt relieved.

"It still feels good to be back home."

"What you gonna name the baby, Gingee?" Another friend asked.

The slight mention of her child made her smile. It was her only connection to Kumasi other than the memories.

Ginger swelled with pride, "Going to name him after my mamma's brother. His name was Alprentice."

"Name was who?" A girl questioned out of curiosity. She was younger than the rest but she came off more mature from her appearance.

Big Tasha cut in and answered sharp and coldly, "Alprentice, Doll-face. Al-pren-tice."

Ginger continued, "I'll nickname him 'Prince', 'cause he is going to be a for-real African prince," looking down at her ever growing stomach.

The first girl almost dropped her fork on the ground, "For true? Naw… put that on sump'in!"

"It's a fact. My husband's father is King of the Zulu tribe back in Africa."

"What?" She exclaimed, with wide eyes.

Everyone was astounded. They leaned in further, sitting on the edge of their seats with their mouths gaped open in disbelief. This was something they heard in movies. Only Ginger wasn't Eddie Murphy and she went to Africa versus the other way around.

"Gingee, what if it's a girl?" Big Tasha asked, with chips in hand, snacking away.

"Oh, it's a boy. I'm so sure…I hadn't even considered a girl's name," Ginger smirked with confidence, tracing her finger along her engorged belly button through the tribal dress she wore home.

Big Tasha kept the conversation going, she was full of questions. Her imagination and curiosity ran wild each day that passed without Ginger. She could finally sit her down and get her to paint the picture she had envisioned for months.

"What are people like?...How did ya feel when you touched down over there?"

Ginger took her time and answered slowly, "Pretty much like here with a lot of different nationalities and what not. Mostly Blacks, but the Whites run everything…but anyway, it was kinda strange. I had this 'I-been-here-before' feeling in my gut."

She hadn't really talked about her experience yet. This was her first time, but she seemed to have triggered their interest because they all looked in awe. No one from their neighborhood had ever gone that far around the world and returned with a story to tell. Most of the stories told were traced within a ten-mile radius.

A boy within earshot interrupted them as he walked up on the girls, rubbing his stomach, "Mus'ta got good 'cause you brought that feeling back with you," laughing.

"Forget you." Ginger said, gleefully.

"Yeah…go on with that." Big Tasha interrupted, "You and yo' good observing ass!"

He brushed her comment off and motioned to greet the guest of honor. Tattoo covered arms extended to hug Ginger, "You know I'm joking. I ain't got nothing' but love and respect for ya," he said, smiling.

Ginger smiled back, she recalled a few of his crazy antics when they were younger and realized, he hadn't changed a bit. Before he stepped away to mingle throughout the party, he stopped in front of Big Tasha.

"Ain't nothing' but love for your big fine ass, too."

Big Tasha swatted him away like a fly, "Lil brother, please!" with disgust smeared on her face.

The girls resumed their conversation. They knew it wouldn't be too long before they were interrupted again. The backyard was moving like a machine, people were constantly coming and going. Family and friends would approach Ginger at different times throughout the night. It seemed as if they were in rotation and everyone read from the same script.

They thought they had seen just about everyone, until the two entered. Big Tasha was surprised when she spotted them walking up, "Gingee!... Here comes Lil Bit and D'Zine. And they packing presents."

Ginger and Big Tasha watched their every move with an untrusting eye. Every step was monitored as Lil Bit and D'Zine set their gifts on the picnic table and walked over to hug Ginger. Ginger obliged with stiff uncertainty. Big Tasha eyed the situation like a magnifying glass, cautious for any strange movements or suspicious activity.

Their embrace didn't settle the air. After they hugged, the tension was so tight that D'Zine just blurted it out, "I'm sorry for what I did."

Lil Bit was close behind and had a little more to say, "Me too, Gingee...I hope you can forgive. We been knowing one another most of our lives and it wouldn't make much sense to walk around rolling eyes at each other.

"Yep...I feel the same way," D'Zine added, "and hope you do too."

"I do. And I still love both of ya'll like sisters. We didn't always see eye-to-eye, but I never had hatred for either one of you." Pent up emotions and hormones caused Ginger's next words to be joined by tears, "It now feels good to let the love flow and put the past behind us. The world is hostile enough, we don't need to enhance it. I don't want my child to inherit any hatred that is carried on by me."

87

"We understand. We hear you been through a gang of pain." D'Zine said solemnly, dropping her head in guilt.

Big Tasha couldn't be happier from what she was hearing, "Hell yeah!" she shouted joyfully. "...I don't know what done got into you bitches, but unity is good among us."

From the rear yard, Dynasty approached the party dressed in a long pants suit. A contrasting silk scarf on top of her head flowed with each dignified step. She smiled upon eyesight of the girls.

Ginger noticed her from afar, "Is that Dynasty?"

"Yeah, girl..." Lil Bit sucked her teeth and delivered the news, "she's a Muslim now."

"Really?" Ginger asked, surprised.

"She don't hang with us like back in da days. We still talk and stuff you know," D'Zine hunched her shoulders, "but we don't kick it."

"Right. We be tossing conversation around. But she don't bang no mo'." Lil Bit said, pointing to the colored bandana tied around her forehead. "It's good though 'cause she don't try to force her beliefs on us."

D'Zine went to grab an extra chair, and walked back over without missing a beat, "She kinda drops things on our mind and leaves it. She's still Dynasty. She might slip and cuss now and then. I look at her and she says the religion is perfect, she ain't".

"After her recovery she started going with some of the brothers that come every Friday to take anyone without a ride to their meeting. To me, it seems like it changed her a lot. But it's all to the good," Big Tasha added.

By the time Dynasty passed the DJ table and made her way over to them, Ginger had received a full debrief on the new Dynasty. She was about to see the changes for herself firsthand. The cordial acts that followed were laced in normalcy. They all stood, greeted each other and embraced.

Dynasty hugged Ginger with humility resting at her fingertips, "The weight of what I did to you has been lifted. But it won't be all the way off until I formally apologize to you. The Creator forgives and I pray daily that you will also forgive me and put our differences aside."

"Hatred only breeds hatred. My husband tried fighting fire with fire and paid dearly with his life." Ginger uttered, hanging her head. The thought was still too heavy to bear. She looked back at the girls with sincerity in her eyes, " Like I told D'Zine and Lil Bit, we don't need to live with grudges. I forgive you, Dynasty."

"Al-hum-du-Allah…that means praise God. I always thank Him first," Dynasty said joyfully. She shed a slight giggle, "I know it sounds strange coming from me 'cause your recollection was of the old Dynasty. But now I look at life with a conscious difference."

Ginger was taken aback by her authenticity. Everyone felt warm vibes floating around. Peace has been made.

Big Tasha stood up and roared, "Well good then! Let's get something to eat."

The girls walked as a unit to the other side of the backyard. They were on a brand new path, reunited and resolved. Time had healed their wounds and ultimately changed the trajectory of their lives paths. Now they were about to share their first meal with one another. As symbolic as that seemed, they were still being interrupted with unwanted entertainment from the guys that came in and out.

A group of homeboys met the girls at the buffet table. The biggest of them was named Large, a hefty teen with huge eyes and a confidence level to match. He boldly slid in front of Big Tasha and tugged at his crotch.

"Tasha...you better put a rush on that lotto ticket."

Big Tasha looked into him with curiosity, "What lotto ticket?"

"The one you shoulda copped, 'cause today is definitely your day. It got to be. I'm free, available, and willing to accept you," licking his lips. He was relatively tall for his age and rather thick. He snickered and some of the boys in the back high-fived each other.

"Don't fade his vulgar ass, Tasha!" Lil Bit yelled, agitated. "He always grabbing at his lil shit."

Tasha played it cool, "Nawwh...He already knows I got a serious thing for his nasty ass. That's why he does what he does."

She turned to a sneering Large, "I got to eat first. Then it's on."

"Well go ahead on, Tasha." D'Zine said, laughing.

Everyone circled around the aluminum pans filled with macaroni and cheese, greens, barbeque, burgers, hot dogs, Mrs. Davis' famous fried chicken and more. Hefty servings were gathered before everyone sat down at a nearby table. The girls were bent over plates, eating and talking. One of the boys from Large's group, a wiry-looking kid named Wolf, shuffled over to the girls.

"Hello, Wolf. How have you been? And where is your sister?" Ginger asked, reaching for a bottle of water.

"Chillin' like a villain. Peaches is at the house. Got some kinda girl sickness. She cussed me out and told me to leave her alone."

The girls giggled, they were all too familiar. Another boy from the group, with the self-proclaimed moniker of Lil Daddy, stepped up to their table. His name was fitting considering he looked as if he missed a few growth spurts. He eyeballed Lil Bit until he got close on her face, raising both his arms in a fighting position.

"Yeah!...What's up Lil Bit?" Lil Daddy asked, probing her.

Lil Bit cocked her head to the side, "You might be going up, up and away if you don't lower them arms."

"I'm getting tired of you shaking me off every time I get at 'cha" Lil Daddy exclaimed, trying to reach for her. She had been his crush for a while. Not by coincidence, she was just about the only girl in the neighborhood who was actually shorter than him.

Lil Bit was disgusted and snatched away, "Don't even try it, Lil Daddy."

He frowned and squinted an eye at D'Zine, moving to his next victim.

"Don't even go there!" D'Zine responded swiftly.

And before he could shift his focus on Dynasty, she intercepted, "I can't afford the luxury of an idle moment laced with negativity."

He got shut down one after the other. Ginger was the last of the bunch. But even a blind man could see that she was unavailable. He didn't stand a chance, and he knew it.

"Damn! I see you been claimed already, Gingee," observing her obvious pregnancy. He finally gave it up, "...ya'll missing out."

Those words were like magic to the girls. Lil Bit was relieved, "I'm so thrilled."

"And please miss me from now on." D'Zine said, slapping palms with Lil Bit. They all broke into laughter. What sounded like chuckles to people passing by was the echo of humiliation to Lil Daddy.

He turned to his posse with clenched jaws and a bruised ego, "Let's get on up. There are more females over there. They might have some sense."

"Yeah…I can see these here done feel smooth out they tree. Soon as we trip to another set and get with other dames, they wants to cop attitudes and beat 'em down," one of the boys added, with a backwards hat and crossed arms.

The girls smiled without a rebuttal. The guys stepped away and flounced over to the other gathering of young women around their age.

***

Captain Starks and Officer Faulk anxiously waited next to their vehicles. The captain impatiently checked his wrist-watch every few minutes. Finally, something came about in the distance.

Officer Faulk saw the headlights through the bushes, "Here the Sarge comes now, Captain."

They watched Sergeant Burger's car jet up the winding road, leading to their meeting spot in the Hollywood Hills. The vehicle skidded to a halt under the night's sky.

The sergeant leaped out in a hurry, nearly out of breathe, "Sorry I'm late, Captain…got caught up in traffic."

The captain chastised him with his eyes, snapped his head around and walked away from the parked cars. Officer Faulk and Sergeant Burger rushed to catch up. They strutted down an incline to the usual opening.

"Excellent news, gentlemen," Captain Starks spoke calmly. "Our operation is back in effect."

Electricity flowed through them. Sergeant Burger nearly jumped in the air, "Great damn news!" He had been waiting for this moment since it had been called off, "…We had to kinda back off from the forest, huh, Captain?"

"Something like that." Captain Starks retorted.

Officer Faulk's eyes grew, "Couldn't have come any fucking sooner! Planting dope and guns was too mild."

Captain Starks proceeded back to his truck, "Very well. Use precaution. I'll be in contact."

They couldn't be more ecstatic. They were given the green light to continue their dark mission. Coincidentally, it was the same night Ginger returned to town.

\*\*\*

Ginger and her mother slumped into their kitchen seats, exhausted from the party. The table in front of them was covered with leftovers and a few unopened gifts, remnants of a good night. Now that they could finally wind down, Mrs. Davis couldn't be happier. She was proud of the turnout and most importantly, Ginger was home.

"That was some homecoming for you, Gingee. I had done forgot most of those kids. Lawd I…I mean each and everyone in these here projects came by. Some stayed and some passed through bidding their hellos', but they all came."

"You're just about right, Momma. I had forgotten a lot of them myself. I knew the faces, but some names slipped me. I was overwhelmed."

"You been through a lot child and I know you're tired out. I sure am." Mrs. Davis got up and stretched out her limbs, "I'm going to bed and you should too. The dishes are done. Mother James and some of my church sisters are coming in the morning to help me tidy everything up. We'll talk tomorrow."

Ginger stood and gave her mother a kiss goodnight. She hadn't done this in months and it pleased her to do so. "Night, Momma."

Later that night, the moon shined over Ginger's restless body. The depths of dreamland encapsulated her as she tossed and turned. Images of Kumai's smiling face warmed her. Deep into slumber, her body seemed to come to peace for a moment. But then, the dream slipped into a nightmare. She walked to the back porch and saw Kumasi and his companions sprawled lifelessly on the ground. If that wasn't enough, the visions in her dream faded to the laughing faces of Captain Starks, Sergeant Burger and Officer Faulk as a whirlwind in her mind. They looked more real than ever.

Ginger instantly awakened. Covers were flung off. She sat up in the bed and looked around with fearful eyes. Assured she experienced a dream, her body slowly laid down and the covers crept back up to her shoulders. It was just a dream, we're ok…it was just a dream. She held her unborn child in the cradle of her hands and drifted back off to sleep.

She didn't want to admit it or tell anyone but her subconscious was deeply affected. The fear of what she saw in that abandoned parking lot froze her to the bones. Her mind played tricks on her while she slept. And strangely, Kumasi was a victim of the very same crime she bore witness to. The domino effect.

# Chapter 13

## *NEW LIFE, NEW LAWS*

After their reunion at Ginger's welcome home party, the girls seemed to hit it off. This time, things were different. They weren't lurking enemies, but friends. As time went on, their relationships grew along with Ginger's womb. They graciously acclimated her and the unborn prince back into the neighborhood.

When she was fully-blossomed, Ginger wobbled with the weight of her expectancy. Dynasty and Big Tasha accompanied her as they walked and talked with hand and arm gestures, laughing amid ghetto highlights. Before Ginger could react to the last joke, she felt something moist in between her legs. Instinctively, she knew it was time. The prince was coming.

With a nurse escort, a smiling Ginger and her wrapped newborn were pushed in a wheelchair to an awaiting vehicle. Ginger's mother and two of her church sisters waited from the car in the hospital parking lot with jubilant enthusiasm. They greeted with hugs and assisted Ginger into the ride.

***

Lil Bit, D'Zine, Dynasty and Big Tasha huddled around Ginger's bed, begging for turns to hold the baby. Ginger extended the child to Dynasty. With a tender grip, Dynasty palmed the infant's head. She situated her lips to the baby's ear and began to whisper a rhythmic chant.

"Damn…sister girl," Lil Bit pouted. "What's with all that whispering and shit?"

Dynasty smiled, "I was reciting the Adahn. It's a call to prayer," guiding the child into Lil Bit's awaiting arms.

"Umm hmmm. We feel ya." D'Zine nodded her head, "Don't fully understand. But we fell ya," shrugging her shoulders.

She watched with worry as Lil Bit rocked the baby, "You gonna wake him up, Lil Bit. Let me hold him fo' you do."

Lil Bit cut her eyes, "Alright, Dee…with your impatient ass," and reluctantly passed the child to D'Zine.

D'Zine reached for him with ease, "I knew it was gonna be a boy. I told ya'll." He settled into her arms. She looked down at his angelic smile.

"Yeah, right! If that's the case, ya need to open a fortune-telling shop somewhere." Big Tasha joked, "You didn't know shit. Hurry up and let me hold my Godson."

"Ginger said all of us is Godmothers!" Lil Bit yelled, cutting her off.

"Awhright...cool…But don't get yo' fucking feathers all ruffled out of shape. Come on D'Zine." Big Tasha said.

She relayed the infant to Big Tasha. Big Tasha held the baby up above her head with ham hock arms, "Hey Prince…Boy, you gonna be fine! But don't be too hard on the Lil girls."

The room was consumed with cackles. Their instant reaction startled Prince. The slits over his eyes opened up to a bright room with Big Tasha staring back at them. Pouting was followed with a few whimpers.

Lil Bit crossed her arms, "You done woke him up Tasha."

"Here, Gingee…" Big Tasha nervously rushed to lay him in Ginger's lap, "you know what to do better than me."

It was something about newborns that required such delicacy – their fragile state sparked fear in the inexperienced.

Ginger gently arched his head over her shoulders and patted the small of his back. The girls looked on in awe. The division in the room was apparent; it didn't have to be said. Mothers and those who had yet to taste the depths of childbirth and motherhood.

As if on queue Mrs. Davis entered, "Give that boy to me," reaching out for her grandson. "Probably needs to be changed. You can all take a break. Momma gonna take care of him." She rocked and bounced him back to sleep before Lil Bit could shut the door behind them.

\*\*\*

Richard Allan Russell stood on the square…slim and straight, as he did when he addressed a jury. He was at his best this morning, inside the law firm's boardroom. His demeanor commanded attention. His colleagues were all ears. Rough copper toned skin disclosed the beach retreats, yacht parties and outdoorsman in him. Silver-streaked hair was worn with manicured ease. Soft blue eyes balanced the ruggedness. An articulate tongue was as flawless as the pure-white porcelain implants that highlighted his award-winning smile.

"Next on the agenda, Counsel, pertains specifically to attorneys Lakewood, Stein, Johnston and McKinney. With regard to the personal injuries pending, it is prudent to request the client be dismissed from the courtroom before any testimony hones in on the tragedy of the injury. The testimony may very well invoke sympathy in jury members…but at dynamic physical cost to the client. Sympathy may not meet the mark. Consider the employment of empathy. A qualified witness who has suffered a similar injury. If possible, shield the client's injuries from the jury."

Richard steadily walked back and forth, "Consistent exposure through the course of the trial can cause insensitivity. I know it sounds melodramatic. I know it works."

He swayed to the wet bar. All eyes followed. After a hefty swig of purified water, he returned to the head of the board table, "Recall the initial shock of viewing the "Phantom of the Opera." Look! You want to see the Phantom declared prior to peeling his protective mask. 'See! Feast your eyes, glut your soul on my cursed ugliness!' Make the jury live in expectation and dread of what they will see. By all means, comfort our clients…a soft touch…stated with 'This can't be easy for you.' If a client has a clinical detachment, subpoena the plastic surgeon to expose the extent of an injury in greater detail."

He cleared his throat, "In closing argument, it is imperative to reveal that the cost of surgery does not cover the psych trauma. The restoration of prior quality of life, quote some literary works cited from others pertaining to the face, the ear, the arm or whatever body part that is relevant. Help them to empathize. The jury will remember Quasimodo. Hold a mirror in front of the jury. Ask them to look at their appearances and consider the client's disfigurement."

Russell checked his watch and concluded the meeting; his thirst to admonish had been quenched, "Gentlemen, I hope you take notes. Let us forge on the day with a winning attitude. I have a court appearance."

"Notification by bulletin shall inform you of the exact date of our monthly early morning meeting. Thank you very much," closing out with grace.

*** 

Ginger screamed out in reaction to another nightmare. Her mother overheard the frantic sound from her room and jumped out the bed. She flung the door open and rushed to her bedside, "You alright, Gingee?" she asked feverishly.

Ginger was so groggy she could barely put the words together, "Yes, Momma. I'm okay." Her mother wiped Ginger's brow and patted the sweat from her forehead. "You're alright now baby…but something is troubling you." She looked with deep concern, "Guess you been through a lot at too young an age. But the Lawd won't put no mo' on you than you can bear. You'll be alright."

"I trust I will Momma…but when? My husband's and other faces keep coming back." Ginger uttered before looking away. She kept trying to erase the pain but the nightmares were becoming more frequent. Haunting her.

Mrs. Davis could tell her daughter was carrying a burden. This troubled her and she wanted to know more, "What other faces, Gingee?"

Ginger tried to dismiss it but she hadn't really told anyone about this, "Just faces…I'm not sure why. I have an idea, but I'm not certain…I'll talk later."

Mrs. Davis gave her one last tuck and a kiss on the cheek, "That's right. You go on back to sleep. Don't worry none. I suggest that you take that job you been talking 'bout. Might help take those faces out yo' head."

"Thank you, Momma. I love you, good night." Ginger turned over and cuddled into the bed.

Her mother walked out and gave her one last look, "Love you too, good night."

*** 

From a mahogany desktop, Vicky Morales, a petite bleached-blonde secretary with marble-green eyes and a cocky attitude, lifted her body and flounced over to the lounge couch where Ginger had been sitting most of the morning. Ginger was looking out the huge window that nested on the tenth floor of the law office, daydreaming as the afternoon sunshine peeked through the glass and onto her face. She was almost startled when Vicky walked up and lightly tapped her on the shoulder.

"Do you have a vehicle, Mrs. Kamuzu?" Vicky asked, skipping past the polite greeting and getting straight to business.

Ginger shook her head, "No, I sure don't."

"I was afraid of that." Vicky said blandly, "Will you please come with me," heading towards the main hallway. "Mr. Russell apologizes for having you waiting all morning. He was abruptly placed on the afternoon calendar. I have been instructed to drive you to the courthouse on my lunch hour. I guess it's urgent."

Sensing her arrogance, Ginger spoke with a sharp tongue that matched Vicky's unnecessary tone, "I'm not what you call thrilled about sitting here for hours either. Nevertheless, I apologize for inconveniencing you."

Out of more fear that Mr. Russell would get wind of her detected disposition than sympathy for Ginger's situation, she altered her mood with a counterfeit smile, "Oh no! By all means, you are in no way inconveniencing me."

"Please forgive the insinuation. Come on, honey…let's get going." Vicky motioned for Ginger to walk with her. Heels clicked against marble floors. They approached two huge wooden doors with silver handles where a very muscular guard waited out front.

When they entered, Ginger and Vicky took their seats at the rear of the courtroom. They kept quiet and stooped low because court was currently in-session. Vicky used discretion to point out her boss, only Ginger could see her finger projecting in front of them.

"That's Mr. Russell addressing the bench."

Ginger nodded. She focused on the attorney. The relation to Robbie was evident. And their names weren't too far off either.

Russell faced the judge, "In conclusion, your Honor, with accord to the common law rule, one cannot be convicted of receiving stolen goods when the actual physical possession of stolen goods has been recovered by their owner or his agent before delivery to the intended receiver. Furthermore, the term 'agent' means any person with a right to possess or control over the goods. A leading case on point is People v. Smith, U.S. v. Coven. Need I add Coppertori v. U.S.?"

The judge hesitated to answer. He scanned through reports and flipped through a few pages in his law books. Over the top of his bifocals he peered at Russell, the defendant, and back to the reports. A grumbling sound led his pathway before speaking.

"You have covered a sufficient amount of area, Mr. Russell."

"Thank you, your Honor."

The judge adjusted his glasses, "When the actual physical possession of stolen property has been recovered by the owner or his agent, its character as stolen property is lost, and the subsequent delivery of the property by the owner or agent to a particeps criminis, for the purpose of entrapping him as the receiver of stolen goods does not establish the crime, for in a legal sense he does not receive stolen property. Case dismissed."

Directly following court, Russell treated the two of them to a nice lunch downtown. Vicky rushed to make reservations on their ride over. Once they arrived, the hostess sat them by a window that overlooked the city.

After Russell adjusted his utensils to perfection, he looked up from the table, "I feel as though I have known you much more than an hour Ginger. Robbie is very thorough with every detail."

Ginger agreed, "I know. She really is," reaching for the menu of the restaurant. She was in the courthouse for so long that it had been hours since she'd eaten.

Russell decided to cut to the chase, no holds barred. He simply wasn't the lackadaisical type of guy. It was in his profession. His personality was all about business. It was his nature, through and through.

"Let's get right to the meat of the matter. You need a job. I do not have a position for you, but I will create one. I love to teach, as you shall learn. Some people go through life making their own chances…Some have them presented to them…Still, some never acquire any. I am going to give you one. Not two. Just one. What you do with it is up to you. Seize it with vigor…," squeezing his fingers into a solid fist.

"You may never get another in life. Now, did you pay attention to what was going on in the courtroom?" he asked.

The intensity he felt about success and what he displayed in the courtroom was captivating, this drew Ginger closer. The career she always wanted was right in front of her eyes.

"Yes, I did. I don't know the specifics, but it had something to do with stolen property. More so, it was about your client being tricked into the possession of it."

"You backed your defense up with examples of other cases that were similar. Am I correct?" Ginger asked, wanting to make a good impression. Although nepotism got her the job, her intellect and passion would keep it.

Russell learned in, his tie pressed against the table, "You amaze me. Keep talking."

Ginger put the menu down for a moment, "The judge didn't want to dismiss the case but I don't think he had much of a choice."

Russell laced his smile an enticing charm. He was intrigued and leaned in further, "Oh, but he did. He could have rendered a conviction with knowledge that a higher court is more of an authoritative position to make the call. Some like to flex their authority to the max and make the call themselves. The judge we had was one of those."

He backed from the table to relieve himself from his fitted navy blazer, "Besides, we golf and socialize with one another. I was within the realm of law so he was able to decide in our favor. But trust me…I owe him one."

"I'm sure you will love having Ginger aboard. Some of your duties will no doubt be lifted." Russell said, addressing his secretary.

She smiled without comment.

Ginger interjected, "I'm the one who will love it," darting her eyes over to Vicky, "Vicky was so very cordial and professional. I'm sure the rest of your staff are equally warm-hearted."

"The offer sets very comfortable with me, Mr. Russell. Thank you and Robbie so very much." Ginger extended her hand, closing out a successful unofficial interview.

Russell did the same and sealed the deal with a creased tie and enthusiastic smile, "That's much better. And you are welcome."

***

Struggling through a busy corridor with a score of sleepless nights etched across her face, an elderly White woman paused at each door in a panic. Blistered eyes strained to read nameplates on the wall of the police headquarters. She proceeded. Finally, a nameplate read Captain John Starks.

The elderly woman sat in the captain's office. She was groped with a stout, rotund Hispanic lady around thirty, two young black teens under drinking age who kept squirming in their seats, and a late-age Caucasian gentleman in a devout state of attention.

Captain Starks closed his paperwork and addressed the group while sitting behind his desk, "…As we conclude, dear citizens, stay mindful of the points we have discussed. Read the pamphlets provided. And fill out the victim of crime applications. If you meet the requirements, the state shall issue compensation. Your personal loses and/or medical expenses."

The elderly woman stood up and leaned against her cane, "Thank you, Captain Starks, but as you know…I myself was not victimized." Her voice began to crack, "My grandson is the one that remains paralyzed by the bullets of the robbers."

The captain sighed, this wasn't the best part of the job. "I understand and you have my deepest sympathy. You are his guardian, Mrs. McAllister. Thus, meeting eligibility."

"The collision that derived from the police pursuit totaled my vehicle. Do I mention that with my medical bill?" The Black girl asked, extending the question and answer period.

The captain got up from the desk and walked around to be closer to the group, "Add everything, Miss Barnes. This is a new program. I have not received a lot of feedback. For now, I would advise you to include everything resulting from the incident."

"Excuse me, sir," the Hispanic woman chimed in, "how long will these here take? I lost everything, you know. My money. My husband, my everything." Emotions got the best of her and she released a few silent tears.

The captain did his best to show sympathy, "Trust me. I know. You people are five out of hundreds that are inflicted daily. This program was implemented to provide a measure of relief. Please follow the written instructions. Allow the wheels of progress to rotate."

"Thank you very much, Captain." The gentleman said, satisfied with the outcome.

"Thank the Department, Mr. Holland. Now, if there are no other questions, we shall dismiss." He hawked the room with a professional smile, "Those of you whose perpetrators are still at large, please continue to work with the investigators."

\*\*\*

Captain Starks met with his superior, Chief Howard Bates, in the police parking lot later that day.

As they approached their vehicles, the chief asked, "How's it going, Starks?"

"Excellent, Howard, and yourself?" Captain Starks retorted.

The chief sat back on the hood of his car, "Same ol' soup. It doesn't end. All we can do is take a bite out here and there. Crime is like tuberculosis. You can't cure it. You arrest it. If you don't keep it at bay, it'll run rampant and take control."

Captain Starks drummed his fingers along his chin, contemplating his disagreement, "I differ. I believe we can eliminate it."

"Don't get me wrong," Chief Bates put his hands up defensively, "That is the ultimate goal. But don't kid yourself either. The prize is in containment. And what the hell, crime keeps a chicken in the pot and a car in the garage."

"There is some merit in that statement."

Chief Bates fired back, "Damn right there is!"

Captain Starks looked towards the building briefly thinking about what was next on the agenda.

"How're you adapting to the new position?" The chief asked, unlocking his car door.

Captain Starks rubbed his hands together, "Very smoothly, Howard. Thank you for the promotion. I enjoy assisting all victims of crime."

Chief Bates gave him a thumb's up, "Very good. We have a certain image to uphold," bending down into the driver's seat. The door slammed. He smiled and gave the 'a-ok' signal before driving off.

***

Captain Starks, Officer Faulk and Sergeant Burger surrounded a small table covered with beer chips. Captain Starks hosted tonight's gathering with a celebration in mind.

He raised his drink in the air, "Congratulations, men! We are gaining a sizeable edge on our mission. Gang-related crime is at an all-time high. The body count mounts."

Faulk popped open another beer can, "Cheers to that!" and joined his arm alongside the captain and Sergeant Burger for a toast.

After they swallowed the deep IPA, Sergeant Burger sat his drink down with a firm grip on the can, "Say, Captain, how do you handle helping those Blacks and Mexicans? I just can't see it."

"No shit…I couldn't help 'em…Victims or not" Officer Faulk agreed.

The captain cut a crafty smile. Sharply, his expression transformed to a fiendish frown, "That is precisely why there are foot soldiers and there are generals. Neither of you are equipped to shield the hatred. I can mask the vile taste they put in my mouth."

He took a huge gulp that sloppily spilled along his hands and around his mouth. He wiped it away with the sleeve of his uniform. "Abundant strength conceals my inner feelings. Strength you both need to muster. Strive for a degree in deception."

He belted out with thunderous laughter. Officer Faulk and Sergeant Burger gazed at one another with a blend of bewilderment and betrayal. They didn't know the truth behind their entire regime rested on the captain's secret dealings with those of a higher pay grade. His cousin was up for office and his entire campaign platform was based on gentrifying the neighborhoods through housing development and reconstruction. The quickest way to do that was to free up the rented space. Captain Starks was tasked with organizing a small group to quicken the pace with coercion, fabricated gang violence, conspiracy, and murder.

\*\*\*

Ginger toured through the firm with two young paralegals: Marshall Jonathan Phelps, a jean-and-loafer-wearing blond, and a nerdy-looking Black kid named Herman Thomas.

The three of them entered the firm's law library early that morning. It was packed everyday of the week, but the mornings were slow because most attorneys reviewed their material at night before court the next day.

Marshall pointed to a row of seats in the study area, "And this is where we spend most of our time."

Ginger scanned the room. Her eyes jumped from books to tables and shelves filled with terminology. It was a lot to take in. But she was fascinated.

While she looked around, the guys decided they had seen enough thus far and choose to rest at one of the long tables. Before Ginger could sit down, Herman saw the look on her face. He could sense she was feeling overwhelmed.

"Do not allow the vastness to intimidate you, Ginger."

"No, don't do that." Marshall said, picking up on it too. "This room will shrink after a few weeks," sitting down in a chair.

"Actually, I'm intrigued." Ginger said.

The young men took a questionable look at one another. She had them fooled.

"Psyche. Just kidding. I sure hope it does."

Herman liked her sense of humor. It was a nice characteristic to have working under the stress of this job. He was happy she had become one of his colleagues.

"Mr. Russell has instructed us to shed as much insight as possible upon you."

"He will groom you as well." Marshall added, "You can bank on that. Don't sweat. Everything will fall into place. It's a breeze."

"Is this your full-time position?" Ginger asked, fingering one of the books in front of her that someone left from the night before.

"For the time being." Jonathan said. "We both attend law school at night. You'll soon see less of us."

She casted her attention to Herman, "So you're going to become a lawyer as well?"

Herman lifted his glasses with the tip of his finger and positioned them firmly on his face, "That is the projection," responding modestly.

"The best of luck to you both."

Herman smiled, "Why thank you."

"Ditto." Jonathan added.

The next sequence of time was filled with the three of them in each other's presence. They explored the ins and outs of the library. And the ins and outs of each other's personalities. They spent so much time together it was like they were attached at the hip. She thought she had formed a tight bond with the girls in the program, but this was different.

Herman always tried to help Ginger when the opportunity presented itself. In one of their late night study sessions, Herman bent over Ginger's shoulder because she needed to clarify something and he graciously pointed it out. Jonathan and Ginger fought with the copy machine everyday for it to work properly.

They would eat lunch as a threesome in the patio of an Italian restaurant every chance they got. Class with Mr. Russell always included lecturing at the blackboard, pointing with a rod.

One morning, Ginger, Jonathan and Herman shared a snack at the table in the coffee room. They were on the fifth floor of the law firm where they would frequent from time to time. Herman stood up to stretch his legs. He shaped a folded newspaper back together and tossed it on the table.

"Going to the men's room. I'll be back." Herman uttered as he walked off.

Ginger lifted the paper and began to thumb through it. She looked up from one of the pages, "I'm going to miss you guys."

"We'll still be here." Jonathan said flattered, flashing a nerdish grin. "Just a cut in hours. Getting ready for finals."

He expected her to respond but there was a sudden silence that entered the room. When Jonathan looked back at Ginger, her eyes were bulging from their sockets. A tense hand trembled to conceal her mouth that gaped open as wide as a corral gate. Fear was personified in her face.

Ginger coincidentally picked up the newspaper and turned to the page that contained an article heralding the Police Department's new Victim of Crime Program, displaying a photo of Captain Starks.

She pointed to the captain's photo, "Now I know who he is…"

# Chapter 14

## CRACKED CODE

Jonathan and Herman sat attentive in the law firm lunchroom, glued on Ginger. She gave the guys a play-by-play outline of everything that happened as they sat across from her. Their heads tilted in. Their eyes barely blinked. They were holding their breath and hanging on to the edge of their seats.

"And that is my entire life story. The bulk of it is in the past two years."

Jonathan and Herman were speechless.

"So, can I trust you guys, or what? Do you believe me?" Ginger asked as a lump gathering in her throat. She hadn't revealed her deepest secret with anyone, especially not at this level of detail.

Herman's hands nervously rattled on the table, "Yes…That is the reason I am numb."

"Fucking incredible!" Jonathan flew back into his chair and crossed his arms.

"You must swear to secrecy. If it gets out, he'll be alerted." Ginger pleaded, her eyes dashing back and forth between the two.

"And you'll be in real danger." Jonathan whispered, "I won't tell a soul. It's you, me, Herman and these books."

Ginger turned for Herman's reply. She needed to make sure he was on board too.

"By all means. It will not go beyond this room." Herman confirmed with trusting eyes.

"I want them brought to justice, guys, I just don't know where to begin."

Before she could relax herself, she started feeling unstable. Not again. She felt this feeling before, but the captain's picture in the newspaper triggered it once again – a stream of vivid memories. Ginger instantly had another flashback. The familiar whirlwind of Kumasi's face, the captain, the sergeant and the officer swept across her mind. Only this time, she was wide awake.

Jonathan noticed her fading out and tried to bring her back. "Ginger!... What's wrong...are you alright?"

She faintly heard him. Ginger was too deep in. Lost in a daze.

The volume of Jonathan's voice prompted Herman to turn around midway down the hallway and back into the lunchroom. He had left shortly before in route to the bathroom.

"Jonathan...what is the commotion about?" Herman asked, almost out of breathe.

He turned to a trembling Ginger. To her aid they both responded.

Although Herman was borderline panicking, he placed a calming grip on her shoulder, "Hey Ginger!...Snap out of it. You okay?"

She slowly removed her hand that was gripped tightly around her mouth. Stress was paramount between the three.

Jonathan took a deep look into her state of health, "You don't look good, Ginger."

"I'll call the paramedics!" Herman let go of Ginger, fear trailing along his voice.

Ginger motioned for him to halt, extending her palm in front of him, "No, I'm okay...I'll be alright."

Jonathan ran to the water dispenser. He drew a cup and handed it to her. Ginger began gulping it like she had just finished a marathon. Her composure regained after a few more sips and deep breathes.

"Listen fellows. I'm going to reveal something I have held in for a long time. At first it was speculation. Now I'm certain." Ginger sat up in her seat. "It's Captain Starks."

"Don't worry." Jonathan said, trying to keep her calm. "The three of us will come up with a solution. We must."

"We will." Herman appeased.

***

Ginger and Big Tasha sat on her mother's back porch in the projects that night.

"Of course, it's safe with me…and the stars above. Damn, homegirl, this is some heavy-ass shit. Why didn't you tell me before?"

"Didn't share it with anyone. I held back out of fear and uncertainty. I didn't see the actual drive-by. But I saw it in my mind. Couldn't get it out. The blackface was some kind of cover-up and their fear when I saw them manifested the flashbacks. When I saw his face in the paper…"

There was a pregnant pause. It felt like she regained the strength of a thousand moons. At first she was scared, she felt powerless in the face of the officers. But after she faced her worse nightmare with Kumasi, the scene replayed night after night, she figured she didn't have anything to lose. The domino effect would end with her. She would continue what her husband started and risked his life for; only she would do it her way.

"I have to do something."

"We gonna lure these fools into a cross." Big Tasha rubbed her hands together mischievously, "Get 'em in a position and put the ambush down!" Her voice rose.

Ginger knew her friend. And she knew her people. But, she also knew what the police had done and the burden she carried. Despite her experience, she still wanted to do this right.

"No, Tasha. I don't want any violence. I want them on the inside of bars."

"It's yo' call." Big Tasha said reluctantly. "I'm here to help at any cost. And you know it."

***

Ginger, Jonathan and Herman sat at an outdoor table, having lunch. Waiters were walking about the café, taking orders from other guests. They didn't want anyone to hear them so they tried to be as discreet as possible.

Jonathan spoke at a whisper, "I have a close friend. He's very loyal. I didn't give him details. Only that I wanted the captain under surveillance. He is devoutly intrigued with electronic equipment. He's a genius. His primary goal in life is to be a world-class private eye. We should have the other two officers' names in a week or two."

Herman added, "His financial profile renders no information that is out of the norm. I'll continue to check other sources. I have a lengthy list of witnesses to drive-by's over the past year."

"At least it's a start," Ginger drew a long breath. "Maybe by the time we gather all the pieces, we'll come up with a plan. There must be someone or something that can help."

Later that night, Ginger and Herman occupied Jonathan's den. It looked more like a law library then a place to relax. When Jonathan entered, he slapped a legal envelope on a table. The pages bounced against the polished wood. Herman unfolded the metal clips, opened the package and spread photos.

Ginger scattered her eyes along the pictures. Her hands shuffled through the photos, trying to match the faces from her dreams.

"That's them. Those two were with him!" she pointed and yelled out of excitement.

Jonathan reached down and picked up the photo, "It seems that this one...uh, Officer Faulk, and Sergeant Burger here are the only people he saw off duty."

"Did either of you observe today's newspaper?" Herman asked.

"No, I didn't." Jonathan responded, looking quickly at Herman. His anticipation dwindled by the second, "What you got, Herman?"

"Ironically, and sadly I might add," Herman cleared his throat, "another drive-by occurred last night. A dark sedan was involved. Moreso, I have arrived at on similar modus operandi. Most of the incidents where a dark car was involved occurred at house parties. There have been a number of others at street corners, in cars, at nightclubs, parks. But only a few dark sedans were recalled. Moreover, the dark sedan incidents primarily occurred at night."

Ginger scratched her head, thinking deeply and searching for logic, "Perhaps they choose house parties because there is less traffic."

Jonathan began putting the pieces together with her. It was starting to make sense, "That would surely lessen the odds of witnesses. I think you're onto something."

They felt like they were edging closer to the truth.

Herman grew in excitement, "Let's focus on the list of house-party incidents. Maybe someone will be able to I.D. these photos."

"No...That won't work." Ginger uttered, sadly. "They wore blackface, remember?"

"You're right, I totally forgot about that." Jonathan placed his hand on his forehead from exhaustion.

Frustration rose in Herman, he started pacing back and forth. "As it stands, we do not have an actual eyewitness." He placed his hands on his hips, "Ginger's account will never render a conviction in court."

They were back at square one. They had all the evidence, yet no evidence all the same. Each of them knew it. If they were going to take them down, there was more work to be done.

Ginger yawned, "Let's sleep on it. Come on, Herman. Drop me off at home, please."

***

Ginger, Lil Bit, D'Zine, Big Tasha and Wolf's sister, Peaches, strolled through the projects that evening, speaking in a hushed tones. They wanted to be cautious because the neighborhood always had their eyes and ears wide open. The girls couldn't afford anything leaking out before their plan was figured out and set in motion.

Lil Bit strutted over to Ginger, "We got the shit fo' their ass, Gingee."

"Yeah...Peaches done come up with a hell of a plan. Didn't you, girl?" Big Tasha added looking towards her for affirmation.

"True that." Peaches said, returning Big Tasha's glance with a high five. Peaches was like the secret weapon of the crew, but she hadn't been around that long. Finally, her CIA mastermind would come in handy.

"With yo' backwards-talking ass." D'Zine laughed, pointing at Peaches.

"Ease up." Big Tasha commanded. "You know she been talking that way since she came back from Atlanta."

Ginger brushed off their child's play. She was intrigued and needed to know more. It couldn't wait.

"What's up, Peaches? Let me here this plan."

***

Sergeant Burger sat in his squad car, parked on an inner city street. His last pull from a cigarette was drawn, filling his lungs with tobacco. He tossed the bud out the window with a flick of the finger as headlights appeared in the rear view mirror. His eyes caught a glimpse of the vehicle slowly stopping behind him. Once he got the signal, he jumped out and walked to the back of the car.

"Evening, Captain. What ' cha got?" Sergeant Burger asked, leaning down with folded arms against the driver seat window.

Captain Starks cuts to the chase, "Word leaked down about some of Faulk's collars. A lot of complaints filed alleging planting of evidence. Nothing concrete. I do not want Internal Affairs to get involved."

"I know what you mean." Sergeant Burger watched another passing car drive along the road, "Don't need anyone snooping around. Especially top brass."

"Right. Pass it on to Faulk." Captain Starks started his ignition, "We will simply intensify our main missions."

Sergeant Burger leaned back off the window, "That should pacify him."

***

The crew decided to meet in their usual spot that morning in the law firm library.

"Some of my sisters have proposed a plan." Ginger said.

Herman drew closer. Jonathan followed.

"It's a good one. But it won't work." Ginger bit her lip.

Confusion overwhelmed them. "Why won't it?" Jonathan asked.

"Let's hear it and evaluate," Herman suggested, pulling out his notebook.

"Well, in order for it to work we need cooperation from the gangs in the city. My people are sure they can get the Black and Hispanic gangs from the east end of town. But it's no way they can communicate with the same from the west, south and north."

"If the plan will work, we will have to give it a try." Jonathan shrugged his shoulders.

A fearful look overtook Herman, "You are completely out of your element, Jonathan. Do you have any idea what those thugs would do to us?"

"There may not be any other resources for us, Herman." Jonathan exclaimed.

Ginger looked at Herman who was covered in apprehension and back at Jonathan, "I'm willing to give it a try."

Herman's anxiety rose, "Oh God...please help us," while shaking like Elvis Presley.

120

# Chapter 15

*SPREADING THE WORD*

Jonathan's car drove along the inner city streets of the Westside. Ginger guided them through a microcosm filled with ethnic shops and condemned buildings laced with graffiti.

After a few blocks, she pointed to the next street over, "Take a left at the stop light, Jonathan. The park should be in view."

A group of Black teens adorned the sidelines of a basketball court in a local neighborhood park. The men and women watched with sheer delight as two teams pounded the blacktop with rigorous agility. They gave the onlookers a show. A slamdunk by near seven-footer called Treetop, quelled the contest. He had no competition. One team extended open palms. The other dug in their pockets.

"Yeah!...Y'all rush it to the backboard. Regroup and hurry on back. You know you can't fade the Top! Now cough them chips up." Treetop yelled, mocking his competitors while he towered over everyone.

Skillet, a deep chocolate-hued member of the losing squad, stood with sweat rolling off a bald head.

"Ain't no thang…Y'all got lucky," he huffed. "We'll be back at that ass."

Emerging from the crowd, a young dame named Giggles pointed to Jonathan's car as it pulled into the parking lot adjacent to the court. It was a bit too fast for comfort. Everyone on the court turned to look. Suspicion glared through their eyes like lasers.

Giggles squinted, "Hey, ya'll. Peep that."

Like magic, weapons surfaced. They rushed towards them. In a matter of seconds, the crowd swooped on the car. The occupants piled out with caution.

Ginger opened the door and placed one foot down after the other. She wasn't intimidated in the least bit. Instead, she smiled, "Hello, is Treetop around?"

"And who the fuck wants to know?" Giggles spat harshly.

Ginger cocked her head to the side, "Look, sister-girl. It's about business. No problems."

Giggles looked her up and down for a moment. "The name's Giggles… sister-girl."

Treetop toppled through the crowd, "I'm Tree, what up?"

"We're law students, Treetop." Jonathan took a step forward, "We desperately need your influence."

"Pardon our untimely presence sir. We can make an appointment if you are preoccupied." Herman suggested, trying his best to hide nervous demeanor and find a way out.

His attempt had failed. His weakness had been revealed. Sensing fear like a predator smells blood, Skillet jumped in.

"Check this out buster, I'm Skillet…Fuck the table manners. Tell the man what's on yo' damn mind!"

Herman's nerves had made his lips quiver. Now he was really shaken, "Excuse my haste, Mr. Skillet. I am very sorry."

Before his embarrassment could continue, Ginger took over.

"We've been researching drive-by shootings within the city. We have leads on certain people who are responsible. We need your help to bring them to justice. We've been playing into their hand way too long."

"Yes, we have a plan. But we need gang members to network for it to be successful." Jonathan added.

Treetop reached in his waistband. His hand covered the butt of a gun. It fit like a glove. He tapped the base of it.

"This brings all the justice I need. When a move comes down on us, we know where it comes from. And we deal with it."

"And we don't blend with anyone out another set." Skillet motioned closer, "We handle our own."

"The people we're talking about ain't gang members," Ginger clarified.

"Don't matter. Like ya been told. We take care of our own problems." Treetop smirked, looking down on them with piercing eyes.

"Would you please give it some thought?" Jonathan pleaded.

"Hold it, white boy! Who the fuck you think you are?"

Treetop pointed his finger in Jonathan's face, "First off, ya'll come rolling up here uninvited. That almost gotcha heads blown smooth off. Then ya ask us to help you and them fool-ass wannabes from the other side. I should peel yo' cap with this justice-maker."

"Spare the urkel-looking fool." Skillet laughed. "I like the way the lame calls me Mr. Skillet."

Ginger cleared her throat, speaking with a level of authority they didn't expect. "Ya'll laughing. This is a serious matter. The people we talking about love it when you're at war with your brothers."

"And kill over a color." Jonathan said.

"There ya go. Running ya mouth off. You don't know shit, cracker!" Treetop mocked. The only reason you ain't bloody right now is 'cause ya got enough heart. Mine's big as all outdoors. I don't allow anyone with weakness to be near me. And it's more than a color thang. It's about respect. Y'all got it all twisted. It's about respect."

"Is it true that you kill your own kind if they inadvertently encroach on your neighborhood?" Herman asked, looking away immediately after. He meant to say that in his head, fear struck him when he realized he actually said it out loud and even worse, they heard him.

"That's right!" Treetop yelled with a serious mug. "See how lucky yo' ass is."

"This is our 'hood." Skillet pointed to the concrete beneath them, "Ya get caught out of bounds, ya get taxed!"

"You don't own one brick on this whole block, and you defend it like you get deeds." Ginger sassed, crossing her arms.

Jonathan added to her comment, "You really should focus on purchasing some land somewhere. A home or something you actually own."

Treetop lifted his shirt and pulled out his pistol, "Get in ya car and burn rubber. Get the fuck out of here before it's too late."

Slowly, they inched closer toward Jonathan's car. Their fear subsided when Skillet jokingly pointed to Herman.

"Hold up!...You. Call me Mr. Skillet one mo' time fo' ya go."

"Goodbye, Mr. Skillet." Herman uttered, looking straight ahead in the back seat. He didn't want to make eye contact or stir up any more problems. This time, his plan succeeded. The gangbangers rolled into laughter as Jonathan's car faded.

A little later that day, the crew didn't speak much as they waited in the car for the next destination. Ginger slowly put on her seat belt, "This is hopeless," sounding defeated. "But we pushing on!"

Herman shrugged his shoulders, "Possibly we can accomplish things without them."

Jonathan didn't oblige, "No, we don't know what side of the city they will respond to."

"Maybe we can make them come where we want." Ginger said, rubbing her chin.

"We still need all points covered. Let's head to the Northside. We can't give up?" Jonathan started the car and pulled off.

Every eye casted a suspicious shadow over Ginger, Jonathan and Herman as they entered the Northside pool room. A massive Black kid in sagging pants approached from the bar area a distance away.

As the kid walked up, every couple of steps he had to reach down to pull up his pants that would fall below his waistline, "Afternoon, Officers."

"No...wait a second. We're not the police." Ginger corrected.

He gave an inquisitive look, "How can I tell?"

The trio pulled out identification. They had been out all day with no luck, if this was his only demand, they didn't have a problem. For Ginger, she had grown used to this ask during her time in South Africa. Only this time, the reason for doing so was the exact opposite of why she had to do it over there.

"See...nor do we possess badges." Herman proclaimed, opening his wallet filled with civilian I.D.'s.

After a close inspection, the kid loosened up, "Don't see gats, either. Guess you ain't rollers. Sho' took you for one-times. What's up with y'all?"

"We need to speak with Raven. Can you help us?" Ginger asked.

"And if I can?" He asked, staggering back from them. He was dangling the keys that could unlock the door right in front of their faces.

Herman slid his hand into a pocket and came up with a bill, "Sir, what did you say your name was?"

"I didn't. I'm known as Bruiser."

"My pleasure, Mr. Bruiser. Will this motivate you?" Herman tempted with money at his fingertips.

Jonathan sensed Bruiser's hesitation, "We just want to ask if Raven will help us catch the people who are responsible for drive-by's on this end of town."

Bruiser evaluated the offer. He returned to Herman, "You can't buy me with no dub. Not any amount! Shoot it back in your hip pocket...'cause if ya'll ain't real you gonna get it all took. Your money and your health. You understand!"

"We're on the straight up and up." Ginger said, speaking his language.

"Ya better be!...Wait here." He pointed to the corner adjacent to them.

Bruiser slipped through a back door. Shortly, he returned with a muscular lad in fashionable clothes. His eyes and skin immediately attested to why he was called Raven.

Finally, they had their foot in the door. But they didn't get much further than that. After Raven was debriefed, he had a sense of uncertainty about their tactics.

"So you're saying you know who these fools are...but you won't put me up on 'em?"

"We will at the right time. Right now, we can't." Jonathan said, hoping he would understand.

Ginger clasped her hands together, "Please say you'll have your people cooperate with us."

"Maybe with ya'll. But we ain't got a beef with the other side of town. The reason is, we don't fuck with 'em. No way, shape, form or fashion. If they included...we're out."

"A collective effort could bring about some harmony." Jonathan suggested, knowing unity was the only way to win this war.

Raven stood up from leaning against a pool table and walked closer, "Ya'll don't know what it really is with us. We don't war over no damn colors! The media puts a little extra on every incident. And that little is too much. Most of our disputes are over drug deals gone bad. Territory where they're sold. Debts and things like that. I'm about stacking dollars. The younger up-and-comers might try to put their name in the G-Book of Big every now and then with an attack that ain't got a dollar attached to it. But most of the time it's like I said. It's about legal tender and large livin'. You understand? But if drama is presented, we got mo' drama for they asses."

"Very interesting." Herman tried to process what he just heard, adjusting his glasses to get a better look.

Bruiser started laughing, "Where y'all find this mark?"

"Herman's good people. Jonathan, too. This is all kinda new to them." Ginger corrected.

Raven looked her up and down, "I can see you're cut outta different cloth. Where you come up at?"

"Eastside projects."

"I thought so."

"But I wasn't one who hung out." Ginger said. She felt the need to clean up whatever image he painted about her neighborhood.

"I knew that, too." He continued to look her over. He seemed more intrigued by her character than the tasks at hand.

Raven turned and walked off without a goodbye. After a few steps, he stopped and faced Ginger. For the very first time, he smiled.

"Give Big Tasha warm regards from Raven."

***

The typewriter sang with great momentum. Fingers moved rapidly along the keyboard. Information was researched. Reports were filed. Intense labor was flaunted by Ginger, Jonathan and Herman early in the law firm.

Mr. Russell entered, breaking the silence in the room, "Good morning."

They looked away from their work and returned the greeting.

"For a moment I thought you three were on leave without my knowledge. Haven't seen a lot of either of you lately."

Jonathan set his pen down after an extended pause, "Been in the field, Mr. Russell."

"Yes sir, a lot of interviews on the agenda." Herman added.

This was music to his ears. Russell was proud of their progress and encouraged them all the same.

"Very well. Stay productive."

"Always, Mr. Russell." Ginger said, closing the book in front of her.

*** 

That evening, their extra curricular activities continued. Ginger, Jonathan and Herman sat with a slim Hispanic by the name of Flanco in the nightclub of a Spanish barrio. He was joined by his sidekick, by the handle of Casper, who was dressed in a shirt and brimmed hat.

"I don't think so. If we don't get problems. There won't be none." Flaco said, blandly.

Casper spread his teeth in a smile, "No pedos…no pedos. You know. Not 'witas, baby-girl."

Ginger chose her words carefully. She didn't have the same protection as she did in the other neighborhoods. "A lot of problems have come from people who wanted you to think it was coming from someone else."

Flaco shrugged, "Maybe so."

Casper continued, "We serve whoever. It don't matter."

"It all comes with the territory. I'm Flaco. I'm a gangster." He threw up a few hand signs. "I live a gangster life…comprende? I know what to expect out here. It's mi vida loco."

"Do it for your family that aren't gangsters." Jonathan suggested. "Perhaps you will gain harmony with your rivals. If so, the barrio will be safer for them."

Flaco looked to one of his boys and nodded with approval, "We would welcome that. But we will not get out-drawn, or caught off guard while we wait."

"Will you please consider it, Mr. Flaco? And you, Mr. Casper?" Herman pleaded.

Casper had an even better plan, "I tell you what. When the time comes, you come talk to us. We run the eighties."

"We will throw down, don't want to talk about it until the time comes. Talk is nada!" Flaco spat.

***

The three of them were surrounded by a huge crowd. Most of them girls and guys dressed in Cholo garb. Other people of the neighborhood occupied each corner of the park in the barrio. The shirtless leader stood strong with tattoos on his chest. A girl on one side. A gun on the other.

Herman reached in for a handshake, "Thank you, Mr. Bull." His attempt was regretted almost immediately.

The leader slapped his hand out of the way, "I told you, I'm El Toro!" He yelled in anger, "No fucking 'Mr. Bull'. You two get this puto our of my face. We will help. Now go before I change my mind."

Ginger hurriedly ended the discussion, "Thank you very much."

"Yes, thank you, El Toro." Jonathan was sure to get the name right this time as they walked off.

The introductions and alliances were almost complete. The crew had one final group to pitch to. They drove a good distance and gave the same spiel when they arrived. All went well.

In confidence, outside a social club, four Asian gangsters gave the signal to Ginger, Jonathan and Herman. After they shook hands, the trio walked back to their car parked in the neighborhood. Finally, true progress had been made.

***

Back in the projects, Big Tasha accompanied Ginger while she fed young Prince. Ginger was overly exhausted from the day's events and the challenges they were up against. But like all mothers, she could carry the world on her back and a baby in her arms at the same time. Plus, she had to make this right for the prince. Kumasi would have done anything to protect them. It was now her job to protect him by ridding this community of cancerous systems and ideologies built between the people and the officials they are up against everyday.

Ginger felt like she was working overtime from the law firm, to motherhood and leading this effort. She was always planning and working by day then strategizing with the homies by nightfall.

"I know how to make Large help us." Big Tasha said, motioning to grab Ginger another towel. "Now Bay Brother and Sluggo from Southeast didn't wanna get in with us. Danny Boy is Lil Bit's cousin…so him and Mad Dog convinced them."

Ginger wrapped Prince closer to her and informed Big Tasha about a few updates of her own, "Well, Chino in Chinatown said if it would cut attacks down they were in. Same with El Toro and them. Flaco and his crew will

132

move at the time. No commitment until then. Treetop didn't want to hear it. Neither did Raven. But I think Raven will when I tell him it's the police. By the way…Raven sent extra-sweet regards. What's up with that?"

"Raven used ta live over here way back in the days. I was still in the sandbox." Big Tasha made a childish expression. "Didn't think he remembered me. Hummmm."

Ginger removed Prince from her breast and began burping him, "Anyway, Treetop might hook his mob up if we let him know."

"I know he will. He'll love ta smoke a one-time." Making a mock gun with her fist and shooting in the air, "Gotta make it clear to avoid gunplay."

"Really though. Ginger frowned up her face. That would defeat our purpose. Oh well…whatever…we'll see if he'll join us."

*** 

Jonathan couldn't wait to tell them the news. He called an urgent meeting at his apartment that night.

"My friend has presented some vital information. The parking site for the dark sedan has been located."

This piece of evidence is just what they needed.

"Great!" Ginger exclaimed, smiling from ear to ear. "I knew they wouldn't keep it at the same factory."

"Evidently to avoid being stopped by honest police." Herman laughed at the irony. "If they ever were pulled over, I'm certain they would identify themselves and state that some form of surveillance was in progress.

133

"Also, the car windows are bulletproof," Jonathan noted.

Ginger got up from the couch and started walking about. It was like months of confusion was finally becoming clear. The more she processed, the more it all made sense.

"That would explain why they kept the same car."

With their newfound information, Jonathan knew Ginger had all of the pieces now, "Okay, where do we stand?"

Ginger ripped a piece of paper in her notebook and started drawing maniacally, "We need to have each member set up parties in their neighborhoods. We'll get the addresses and hook fliers up."

The boys had no clue where she was headed. She was still going to work, with a pen in hand, leaning over the table and maneuvering across the pages swiftly.

Herman took a peek at what she was doing. He then realized, "We may have to feed more information to Mr. Raven and Mr. Treetop."

"Right, I was thinking the same thing." Ginger added. "Their hoods must be included. We don't want to miss, hopefully Raven and Tree can agree to a short truce."

Jonathan reminded Ginger, "I know you don't want any weapons or deadly violence but that might be a tall order with these hard core gangsters."

"I know." Ginger sighed. "I just hope we can trick the cops and take them down without gunplay because I know everyone there will be packing heat. Especially Raven and Treetop!"

"No doubt," Jonathan cracked.

Ginger added, "we can't worry about it now. I just want them to live to face life in prison with no chance of ever getting out. That's what I want! But let's stay focused on tying up loose ends and pray the plan works. We need everyone to spread the announcement by word of mouth as well."

Jonathan looked at the map Ginger created, detailing the names of each gang and their leader. Genius.

And then it struck him, "We need everyone to spread the announcement by word of mouth as well."

Ginger backed away from the table and over to the boys on the adjacent couch. She plopped down in between them and placed her arm on each of their shoulders, "Thanks, guys…I could never have gotten this far without you. I love both of you."

"You had that much coming. I was compelled to help." Jonathan said, leading into her embrace.

Herman was just as humbled by her statement, "Any decent person would have done the same."

"Let's not throw a party just yet. We have a ways to go." Jonathan said. And with that, their meeting was adjourned.

\*\*\*

A lanky mid-aged spokesman served a lucid message to a multi-ethnic gathering that expanded to the outer boundaries of a neighborhood park. The rally to eradicate gang violence neared its zenith as the spokesman wrapped up his speech.

"…And I say to you, only a gene or two compose our physical differences. We are all from Adam. Not Eastside, Westside, North or Southside. And to those who belong to gangs…we know we cannot make or force a change."

The spokesman could feel the energy moving. He grew more passionate about his words and leaned in closer to the mic, "You are the ones who have the power to do that. You can transcend the acts of violence and deliver us to peace and harmony. I present a challenge to the leaders. The O.G.'s with influence. Start with yourselves. Let's respect our neighbors. Let's be cordial, helpful, and above all…peaceful. Admonish the younger ones who follow your footsteps. I know what they will say; they'll say you lived yours and they're going to live theirs. So leave them positive example. If the younger ones do as you now do…we will have another repetitious generation; tomorrow we will be in the same condition we are in today. Let's elevate, our human-selves cannot excel to excellence as a people unless we initiate a change. We need to rejuvenate family values. No one can give it to us. We must do it for the enhancement of ourselves."

His eyes paned the crowd as his message faded to their ears. All too focused on him, no one noticed the vice car watching from across the street. Sergeant Burger and Officer Faulk listened from a distance to remain undiscovered. The spokesman's message affected them differently.

SLAP! Officer Faulk slammed his hand on the dashboard.

"You hear that asshole!"

"Yeah…I hear the fuckhead. The bastard has been promoting peace in different sections of town each weekend.." Sergeant Burger kept a steady eye on the crowd while Officer Faulk stressed the situation at hand.

"Well, we're gonna speak to the captain about it."

136

Sergeant Burger kept his cool, "I'm sure he's aware of it. He once said that we only need to create chaos when the streets get too peaceful…"

He paused, "…said the assholes are so full of drugs, alcohol, inferiority and smog that they won't have clear heads long enough to envision what's really going on."

"Smog!...That's a good one for laughs. The bastards got a lot working against them. And that aint enough! I think we need to add weight to their burden," Officer Faulk said, still keeping an eye on the rally.

"Me too. The captain thinks he's got every fucking angle figured out. He doesn't think we're capable of organizing shit."

"I seen that, too. We need to go over his head." Officer Faulk suggested they had both had enough. "Drop his butt a notch or two. He ain't no fucking Einstein here."

Sergeant Burger took his eyes off the crowd and looked Officer Faulk in the eye, "Sounds like a plan. We don't have to wait on his fucking orders."

Officer Faulk began to pant, "Let's get it on!"

***

The next phase was getting the word out. Big Tasha, Lil Bit, Peaches and D'Zine spent hours connecting with the people in the inner city on street corners. In parks. Through alleyways. Everywhere gang members congregated. They whispered. They received nods of approval.

Ginger, Jonathan, and Herman put in some work too. They merged with gang members across the city. Part of the process included written data… giving notes. They had a meeting with Treetop. And met with Raven. Other gang members approached cars. They sat on buses. Whispering silently between them.

Ginger, Herman and Jonathan maneuvered around the print shop. Fliers were purchased. The plan was in full effect.

# Chapter 16

## *DOUBLE TROUBLE*

Officer Faulk and Sergeant Burger huddled around the captain's driver side. They decided to meet in their usual location in Hollywood Hills at dusk.

"I am aware of the weekend rallies. They do not pose any immediate threats." Captain Starks said, leaning further back in his seat. "However, as a measure of safety…we shall defer our activities.

Burger and Faulk gazed at one another with 'I-told-you-so' eyes.

Captain Starks put his car in drive, "I shall contact you."

"Right, Captain." Sergeant Burger tapped the roof of the car.

"Yes, sir." Officer Faulk agreed, backing off from the driver's seat.

The captain saluted them and sped off.

Sergeant Burger waited until he was out of earshot, "We figured that much."

"What he don't know is the streets have a strange air. I'm on patrol more than either of you," Officer Faulk exclaimed, pointing to his chest. "Can't pinpoint it…but something's going on, Sarge."

"Hasn't been a drive-by reported for a few days now. That's fucking odd." Sergeant Burger tightened his lips and scowled his face. "Keep your eyes and ears open."

"I think those rallies have something to do with it." Officer Faulk suggested.

"Maybe."

"We need to strike up the band."

Sergeant Burger displayed a crafty smile, "I think you're onto something that strikes my lil-White fancy."

Officer Faulk grinned deviously, "I'm getting a rush already."

"Let's strike this weekend. Fuck the captain!" Sergeant Burger flicked his middle finger in the air.

Officer Faulk flashed his too, "Yeah – up his sophisticated ass!"

***

Dynasty sat with a cast on her arm, boiling in anger. She thought looking at the stars outside Ginger's bedroom window would take her mind off her frustrations. But it didn't. Ginger and Big Tasha extended comfort as best they could.

"Naw, girl...we know ya wanna be down with us." Big Tasha walked over and squatted down in front of her by the bed, her jeans tightened at the knees. "I know what's in da heart ya got...But 'cha can't."

Ginger added, "No, Dynasty...you need to recover from your accident. We don't know what to expect. It may become physical. You can't risk it."

140

"But I want to give some kind of assistance…Something." Dynasty pleaded. She felt like such a bum. This was a once in a lifetime experience and she was being robbed of it from a trivial arm injury. A soldier who wasn't invited to the battle.

Big Tasha sensed what she was feeling. But she knew they couldn't jeopardize any part of the plan. "We gonna handle it, homegirl."

"We can't allow anything else to happen to you." Ginger gave a very concerning look.

Reluctantly, Dynasty gave in with a faint smile. "Oh well…I see I can't change your minds so we won't drag this on and on. I've been taught that when I see an injustice and can't do anything physical about it, I should speak out against it. If I can't do either…I should pray on it. So, my beloved sisters, my prayers will be with you." Dynasty put her hands together as best she could with the cast and bowed her head slightly.

\*\*\*

The patrol car drove through an intersection of the inner city streets. Traffic was moderate around afternoon when most people were at work. This gave the officers the ability to cruise along and take their time observing even the smallest details on the streets. Officer Faulk and his partner, Wimberly, eyed a poster tacked on a telephone pole.

"Hold up, Wimberly…I've been seeing those posters all over town." Officer Faulk pointed to the sign as they passed by.

"I saw 'em, too. Something about parties this weekend." Wimberly said nonchalantly. He had no idea the level of importance this was to his partner.

Officer Faulk was dead silent. He read the announcement and retained the address. His mind processed the next steps. The outcome. The glory. The high.

Wimberly felt quite the opposite, "Ain't during my shift. I could care less. I'm out for major criminals – murderers, robbers, credible collars."

"Yeah…" Officer Faulk uttered, breaking his silence, "probably a bunch of juvies, might collar someone with a stick or two of weed."

He tried his best to cover up his real intentions.

Wimberly kept riding along and thought nothing of it, "We can pass it on to Juvie Division. Me myself, I'm working on a transfer to Robbery detail."

Perfect he'll never suspect a thing, Officer Faulk quickly smirked to himself. His cover up and perceived lack of interest had worked.

"Right. Don't worry about mentioning the parties. I'll do it. Let's get going…we got a city full of criminals at large."

The police radio squawked out from the speaker with a sense of urgency, there was a robbery in progress…officer down. The vehicle surged with full acceleration. Siren and flashing lights flipped on with a click of the finger. A simulated hand grabbed the mircrophone.

"Four-seventeen responding!...Over." Wimberly responded, excitedly.

Like any other day in their profession, there was always room for the unexpected. It was the nature of their occupation. Urgent response to danger. The black and white car zigzagged through traffic and faded past vehicles.

\*\*\*

Decked out in civilian clothes, Officer Faulk and Sergeant Burger nursed beers at a secluded table in the back of the bar. Their shift on the force had ended but their secondary job had begun.

"Damn if I know…never seen such." Officer Faulk extended a group of fliers to Burger.

Officer Faulk drunkenly flipped through the papers. His intoxication was growing by each gulp. He squeezed the remaining papers in his hand and held it up above face level, "Six fucking parties in different sections of town. All on the same night."

Burger lifted his glass, the swig was long and deep, "Ahh…this is a sweet surprise. They're boasting to be the parties of the year at each location."

"I get you." Officer Faulk sluggishly nodded, "Somebody is sure to get jealous and rain on someone's party."

With glee in their eyes, the men casted grins to each other.

"You damn right…guess who that somebody will be?" Sergeant Burger asked.

Officer Faulk laughed, "How many fucking guesses I got?" he shot back.

Seriousness consumed the mood. Sergeant Burger changed his approach and eased in, "Let's pick two of them."

"All six would suit me just dandy."

"That's interesting." Sergeant Burger groped his chin, "Hummm…what we will do is jot 'em all down. We hit. We move. We play it by ear as we go."

Officer Faulk grew in excitement, "Brilliant fucking strategy, Sarge."

*\*\**

143

The lone dark sedan hummed through back streets, on edge of town long after sunset. A small boy viewed the car as it whipped across an intersection. He entered a phone booth on a mission.

"Right…Couldn't be Southside…they're headed North…up Broadway." The boy whispered through the phone received, trying to keep the glass walls from making an echo. The posters and ad's that covered the booth added to his cover. Every few moments he'd take a look around to make sure the coast was clear and he hadn't been discovered.

Miles later, the lone sedan swung onto another main drag.

A younger teenager watched as the car flew through another intersection later that night. He ran to the phone booth that was on the adjacent block of the poolroom, "They just passed…headed west. Gotta be Westside 'hood."

Ginger anxiously listened on the other line, monitoring the phone in Jonathan's apartment.

"Thanks, Tookie…Alert everyone as planned. Southside and Eastside will be on the way," she said, hanging up the phone.

Her fingers moved in a panic, racing to make another call, "Yes! It's Westside."

The phone slammed with authority. She jumped to her feet. Jonathan and Herman followed out the door. Her fearless approach captivated the boys. They thought she was amazing before, but after this, she shocked them even more. She possessed power and courage, a true woman on a mission. Not some girl with a feeble plan.

Ginger entered the passenger seat of the car. Once everyone got situated, Ginger sharply turned around to update Jonathan and Herman.

"Westside is already on post. I hope all the backups get there in time. Let's go…we can't miss this."

"No way!" Jonathan exclaimed before forcefully driving off.

***

The elusive sedan whipped around a corner and onto another main drag on the Westside. All the while, a long caravan of lowriders blanketed the streets. The multitude of headlights were blinding. Even another group consisting of lowriders. New and old cars converge.

The sedan bended a corner and slowed to a crawl.

***

Ginger's impatience was undiscoverable at first, but now she was on the edge. She tried her best to drive Jonathan's car from the passenger seat. "Cut through the alley ahead…" Ginger directed. "We're almost there!" she urged.

***

Sergeant Burger switched on his turning signal, "I'll take a left on the next residential…you have your position back there?"

"Let's get it on, Sarge."

The sedan loomed around a corner of the residential area on the Westside. The ritual had begun. Lights fell out. It moved slowly. Passing parked lowriders. Officer Faulk waited in the backseat with his gun in hand.

Sergeant Burger looked down a few streets and sensed an eerie feeling, "Street is like a ghost town. Some fucking 'party of the year'. Plenty of cars, though…Just ain't a soul in sight."

145

"They must all be inside. I hear music." Officer Faulk suggested, he noticed the dryness of the streets too. This was quite strange but he didn't want to think too much into it. His finger was burning at the trigger. This was a big night for them and he couldn't let a fearful doubt get in the way of that.

They coasted directly in front of the party house. The sedan stopped.

Sergeant Burger double-checked the address, "This is the target. Some shithead must be giving a speech. Those shadows ain't moving."

"They will in about two seconds." Officer Faulk shouted, releasing that burning sensation with a press of a finger, "Eastside Red here, fools!"

Gunfire from Faulk and Burger peppered the picture window. Glass flew. Shadows fall from sight. Weapons filled with smoke. The sedan squealed toward the exit at the end of the block.

On the corner over, a swift merger of old cars barricaded the exit. The occupants jumped out and spread like a breaking wave.

"What the hell!" Sergeant Burger yelled frantically inside the sedan. He couldn't believe what he was seeing.

Officer Faulk panicked, "Back up…Get out of here!"

The sedan backed up, burning rubber. They hit a parked car trying to flee, spun around and bolted for the opposite exit. Another blockade sealed their path. They were trapped.

Directly above, a police helicopter's light beamed down on the sedan. Sergeant Burger and Officer Faulk were seen bailing out of the car, running between two houses. The helicopter activated backup lights to illuminate the entire block.

From above, they saw hundreds and hundreds of gang members with locked hands. Fingers interlocked, forming a human chain that surrounded the entire block. Faulk and Burger reached a rear yard. The human chain elevated their arms in victory.

Raven's eyes were locked on Treetop, and Tree's were glued on Raven. They were hardcore adversaries, to the bitter end, and had never been that closer to one another. Perhaps, they would never be that united again in life. But, right then and there on this particular night, they were comrades with locked hands and clenched fists.

Officer Faulk and Sergeant Burger's hearts raced as they ran back across the opposite side. The extended human net raised locked fists in jubilant victory. They were trapped once again.

Blacks, Hispanics, and Asians formed every link of the human chain. Jonathan, Ginger, Herman, Big Tasha, Lil Bit, D'Zine, and Giggles held strong alongside others from various hoods. Large, Flaco, Wolf, Lil Daddy, Peaches, and Skillet stood firm and rooted to the asphalt.

Police rapidly converged on the scene. Sergeant Burger and Officer Faulk laid in the middle of the street. Spread-eagle, faces on the ground.

# Chapter 17

## *THE SECRET IS OUT*

Chief Bates' office swarmed like there was a beehive in the middle of police headquarters. Captain Starks and a dozen other personnel brass listened intently as a rage-filled chief vocalized his anger this morning.

"Well, as I fucking live and breathe! I was told that I would see it all." The chief pierced his eyes at everyone in the room, redness growing under his skin.

"I haven't slept since last night's disaster!" He yelled, caffeine seeping through his pores, his eyes strained from restlessness and carried dark bags. "Two fucking nit-wit officers have once again destroyed the department's image. The Mayor and every member of the City Council are riding me like Seabiscuit."

An officer opened the door with an announcement, "The press is here, Chief. Setting up for the conference."

That's exactly what he didn't want to hear right now.

"Get the hell out of here!" Chief Bates yelled with exasperation, "I'll address the press conference whenever I come out!"

The door slammed. The chief snapped back. His heart racing at full speed, he knew the situation couldn't be any worse.

"A lot of good men will have to beat the burden of those two psychos. Ballistics are back. Their weapons were used in too many drive-by's to mention at this time. The fucking evidence is irrefutable."

Again, the door opened. Four men in suits and ties entered with intention. Chief Bates was fed up with the interruptions. Not only did he have to manage this fiasco but he couldn't even get his job done with all of these moving parts.

"Didn't I tell you that I would begin when this briefing is done?"

The men stood, unmoving. They identified themselves and flipped out badges. Those of which were higher ranking than the chief. The first man spoke with a deep voice that struck him off guard.

"Excuse us, sir...but you and your briefing will have to wait. I'm Raymond Chancelor..."

The chief and everyone in the room didn't want to admit it, but they were intimidated. A rare instance. He pointed to his associates and continued.

"This is Mark Grey and Lawrence La Day. We're from Internal Affairs. This is Jack Rollins, he's with the Justice Department."

They turned to Captain Starks, "Captain John Starks, you are under arrest for murder and conspiracy to commit murder." Two of the men grabbed Captain Starks' arms. They handcuffed him without resistance while the first man read him his rights.

149

"You have a right to remain silent. Anything you say can and will be used against you in a court of law. If you cannot afford counsel, a lawyer shall be appointed for you."

The curtain fell down, but the nightmare commenced. He didn't know what was happening. What he feared most...were the legal allegations. Sergeant Burger and Officer Faulk acted on their own, he rationalized. But could he prove it? He knew his fate hinged on Burger and Faulk. He was absolutely, positively correct.

***

Mr. Russell entered the law library of the firm where Ginger, Jonathan and Herman were busy at work.

"Did you kids view today's newspaper?" Mr. Russell asked.

They focused on him with innocent eyes.

"Cops doing drive-by's. That's incredible." He put his hand on his forehead in disbelief, "hard to believe, isn't it?"

"No, not really." Ginger responded, unmoved by the news.

"You always say to expect the unexpected." Jonathan added.

"Anything can..." Herman paused for dramatic effect, "...and will happen in South Central."

"Well...it's never over till jury returns." Mr. Russell said, sprinkling in some of his legal expertise, "But this case will be a swift one. The papers state an overwhelming amount of evidence. The two officers rolled over on their captain...said they were under his order."

"Looks like a cut and dry case. They fell off the edge."

"Oh well." Ginger hunched her shoulders.

Russell exited the room…reading the papers in his hands.

The three rose and slapped high-fives.

"Yes!" Ginger was thrilled. They had really done it. They'd gotten away with it. The take down of power and coercion, with a little ghetto espionage.

Jonathan couldn't help but express his joy when he saw Ginger's reaction, "I'm as happy as you are."

"Thanks again, guys." Ginger was really touched by the entire ordeal but she held her composure as she had always done. "I'm totally lost for words…and words can't express my gratitude."

"Honestly, I thought it would be difficult…" Jonathan closed his notebook, "but it wasn't. Dealing with the gangbangers was the worst part…but I learned a lot."

"Yes…it did come off rather smooth." Ginger glided her hand like she was flying a plane.

Herman rubbed his hands together and licked his lips, "Like butter, baby."

Ginger and Jonathan casted a strange look at one another. They stared at Herman. Then back at each other. Followed by a burst of laughter from all three.

\*\*\*

Ginger carried Prince. Big Tasha, Dynasty, Lil Bit, D'Zine and Peaches joined her. They walked through the projects. Passed a group of boys shooting craps. A small team of young girls practiced dance steps. They approached a basketball game. Passed five girls double-dutching. Another group of skaters flew by. A group of well-dressed Muslim men were passing out books. A calmed normal had returned to the projects.

***

Ginger and her mother walked through Chief Kamuzu's garden in the Zululand of South Africa. She finally convinced Mrs. Davis to join her after months of begging and she was happy she came.

The sun beamed brightly upon them. The chief held Prince, he noticed the resemblance from Kumasi's younger years. It pleased him to know his spirit would truly live on.

They walked. They talked. They laughed.

Ginger finally had a family again and the nightmares were put to bed and never woke up.

THE END…

26829292R00100

Made in the USA
San Bernardino, CA
23 February 2019